Take My Dare

TAKE MY DARE

by J. Kenner

Take My Dare

Print Edition

Cover design: Covers by Rogenna

Published by Martini & Olive

New York Times *bestselling author J. Kenner returns to the smoking hot, emotionally compelling world of the Stark International trilogy that features Jackson Steele, a strong-willed man who goes after what he wants, and Sylvia Brooks, a disciplined woman who's hard to get—and exactly who Jackson needs…*

I've never been happier than I am with Jackson Steele. But I should know better than anyone that happiness always comes at a price …

My life with Jackson is nothing short of perfection. He is my love, my husband, the one man in all the world who makes me feel alive and whole. Our careers are on track. Our family is growing. And the ghosts of our past have been vanquished – or so I believed.

When a wonderful night of sensuality and passion following a masquerade ball turns dark with the news that haunting, horrible photographs of me have surfaced, my old fears and insecurities threaten to knock me down, and it is only within Jackson's arms that I find the strength to endure.

But even Jackson's protection may not be able to save us, because I know my husband well. And he will do whatever it takes—even if it means risking himself—in order to protect our family…

Contains a bonus Steele Short Story, Steal My Heart!

***Take My Dare* is intended for mature audiences.**

Also by J. Kenner

The Stark Trilogy:
Release Me
Claim Me
Complete Me
Anchor Me

Stark Ever After:
Take Me
Have Me
Play My Game
Seduce Me
Unwrap Me
Deepest Kiss
Entice Me
Hold Me

Stark International

Steele Trilogy:
Say My Name
On My Knees
Under My Skin
Steal My Heart (short story)
Take My Dare (novella)

Jamie & Ryan Novellas:
Tame Me
Tempt Me

Dallas & Jane (S.I.N. Trilogy):
Dirtiest Secret
Hottest Mess
Sweetest Taboo

Most Wanted:

Wanted

Heated

Ignited

Also by Julie Kenner

The Protector (Superhero) Series:

The Cat's Fancy (prequel)

Aphrodite's Kiss

Aphrodite's Passion

Aphrodite's Secret

Aphrodite's Flame

Aphrodite's Embrace (novella)

Aphrodite's Delight (novella)

Demon Hunting Soccer Mom Series:

Carpe Demon

California Demon

Demons Are Forever

Deja Demon

The Demon You Know (short story)

Demon Ex Machina

Pax Demonica

Day of the Demons

The Dark Pleasures Series:

Caress of Darkness

Find Me In Darkness

Find Me In Pleasure

Find Me In Passion

Caress of Pleasure

The Blood Lily Chronicles:

Tainted

Torn

Turned

Chapter 1

MORNING ARRIVES BEFORE I'M ready for it, my dreams pushing me from sleep. Not nightmares, thank goodness. Those, I have mostly conquered. Instead, this is a vague dread, a sense of unease, but so amorphous that it dissipates like wisps of clouds when I try to grasp it.

That doesn't matter, though. I'm certain I know the subject of this dream, the reason behind this pervasive apprehension.

My father.

Because this is the day he is being released from prison, paroled early after serving more than two years following his confession of murder. A murder he committed supposedly to protect me, but it was too little too late, and I know damn well that it was not my protection that motivated him, but his own guilt for the hell he put me through when I was a teenager.

I shudder and pull the sheet up to my neck, as if the thin cotton percale will act as armor against my memories. For the last few years, I've tried to open my heart to forgive him. To see him as a penitent who performed a noble sacrifice as payment for my goodwill. But nothing he can do will erase the past. Nothing he says can change reality.

He wounded me, and I will forever bear the scars.

Some girls grow up feeling like princesses, their fathers doting on them, telling them that Daddy will always be there. That no boy will ever be quite good enough for Daddy's little girl. That they are sweet and smart and beautiful and that the world is there for them to conquer. Words spoken with affection and colored by love.

I've known those girls, but I was never one of them. My father tossed me into hell, treating me as a pawn. Or, worse, as currency. My parents doted on my brother Ethan, the fragile little prince. And while I adored him, too, I hated the fact that I was never the princess. I was chattel, and I was destroyed, and the scars of my childhood lingered far too long, creeping into my dreams and stealing my confidence.

But that was then.

That was before Jackson.

Jackson Steele, the man who colors my days and enriches my nights. The man who saw the strength in me. Who held my hand as I battled my fears, and who never gave up on me.

The man I love.

The man who is my husband and the father of my children.

I turn automatically to look at his side of the bed, even though I know he's not there. He was called out of town yesterday morning for an emergency at one of his building sites, and won't return until early afternoon. I press my palm against his pillow, and for a moment, I let myself mourn his absence, knowing that he'd gone only because I had essentially pushed him out the door, insisting that I would be fine by myself. That today wouldn't break me.

But I'm not fine, and I hate that the horror of my past has turned me into a liar.

I want him beside me. No, more than that. I *need* him. *Crave* him. His touch. His power. His passion.

For so long, I've been strong, the worst of my demons battled back. But now my yearning is like a living thing, roused and hungry after a deep hibernation.

I sent Jackson away believing I could handle this without him, and the realization that I was so very wrong makes me feel both small and foolish.

Stop. Dammit, just stop.

With renewed determination, I get out of bed, resolved to shake off the ghosts that are clinging so tenaciously to me this morning.

I move the short distance from the bed to the glass panels that make up the western-most wall of our house in the Pacific Palisades. A glorious Friday morning is just breaking, and I stand there in my short silk nightgown and look out at the vast expanse of manicured lawn and the ocean beyond, watching the vibrant oranges and purples vanquish the pre-dawn gray.

I once told Jackson that I wanted a house in the hills with a rooftop patio, a huge yard, and a view of the ocean. During the day, I wanted to watch the boats as they disappeared beyond the horizon, and at night, I wanted to sit on that patio under an infinite blanket of stars and contemplate the silver moonlight that danced on the cresting waves.

He'd listened to every word, understood every dream. Then he kissed me and told me he'd build me a castle under the stars.

And he did. He really did.

Of course, the fact that he's one of the most famous and successful architects alive helped a bit, and I'd watched as the abstract ideas I'd shared with him sparked a wonderland of possibilities. As smudges on paper became trusses and beams. As dreams became real.

I think that is one of the things I love most about him—the power he has to lasso infinity. To bring imagination to its knees and craft something beautiful from nothing more tangible than the illusive flicker of an idea.

He may have built this house for me, but together we made it a home.

And in point of fact, I'm still not the princess of this castle. That, however, is fine by me.

I turn back to face the interior of the room, smiling as my gaze lands on the tousle-haired little girl curled up in the oversized armchair. She's the real princess, and right now she's sound asleep beneath her favorite blanket, her thumb in her mouth and her dog, Fred, curled up on the rug in front of the chair. Veronica Amelia Steele who, like her father, has stolen my heart completely.

This early in the morning, I'm not surprised she's still asleep. She's staying home from kindergarten today, and so I'd let her play past her bedtime. I'm also not surprised she's in that chair. Though she'd fallen asleep on her father's side of the bed after begging three times for "just one more chapter" from her favorite Magic Treehouse book, she hadn't stayed in the bed. She's adopted the comfy chair as her own private domain, and sometime during the night she moved there as she so often does.

As I watch her sleep, Fred raises his head. He's part corgi and part beagle, with ears that seem just a little too large and a tail that never stops wagging. His mouth opens in a wide yawn, and he turns toward Ronnie before looking back at me, his head cocked as if asking, *Now what?*

"It's okay," I whisper. "Let her sleep. I'm going to go check on the baby."

As if he understands, his head drops down onto his paws, and I leave him to stand sentry over my daughter. I grab the portable baby monitor off the dresser before I pad barefoot down the hall. Ours is the only bedroom on this floor, but there is also a small den that we've turned into a temporary nursery for Jeffery, the other man in my life. He's already a year old, and it amazes me how quickly the days have gone by. Once upon a time, I'd been crippled by the fear of failing as a parent. Now, I can't imagine life without my kids.

I reach the nursery, but hesitate before turning the knob. As much as seeing his sweet face will brighten my morning, I can't deny the allure of a few more minutes of peace—a very rare commodity in our house these days. Jeffrey rarely sleeps past six, but even though it's already six-thirty, I know from the silence of the baby monitor that he hasn't stirred. Open that door, and it'll be all over. But if I go downstairs to the kitchen, I just might have a few quiet moments with my coffee on the back patio before the day begins.

"Soon, little man," I whisper, then back slowly away and move eagerly toward the stairs.

The house is shaped like an H, with the crossbar being the one story section. It features our kitchen, two living areas, the library, and a small gym. The entire western-facing wall is made of sliding glass panels that can be pushed to the side, turning that section into indoor-outdoor living space. The really cool thing about the crossbar is that it forms the foundation for my rooftop patio. A decadent living space with comfortable outdoor furniture, an outdoor kitchen, a fire pit, and a narrow infinity pool.

The uprights of the H contain the home's bedrooms. The kids' and two guest rooms on the ground floor of the southern side with a media room and playroom above them, and Jackson and I on the northern side. Our bedroom and the den-turned-nursery take up the top floor, and our connecting offices fill the lower level.

An exterior staircase spirals down from the balcony off the master bedroom to the rooftop patio, then continues down to the first floor and the flagstone sitting area that flows into the manicured yard. This morning, I forgo those exterior steps in favor of the interior staircase that leads directly to the alcove between the kitchen and breakfast area.

I move slowly and quietly—because now that coffee is on my mind, I'm even more careful not to wake the baby—but I freeze the moment the breakfast area comes into view, my hand flying to my mouth to stifle a surprised little gasp.

Jackson.

He's right there, right in front of me at the breakfast table in threadbare jeans and a plain white T-shirt. He's cradling our son in his lap, his focus entirely on Jeffery as he holds the bottle stable for our sleepy little man.

He hasn't shaved and his clothes are rumpled. I'm guessing he hasn't slept since he left me yesterday, and I know how little sleep he got the night before that. It's clear he's utterly exhausted, and yet there is such a look of tenderness on his face that it makes me want to weep.

For a moment, I stand perfectly still watching him, his dark head bent over the equally dark tufts of our son's hair. The hint of copper in Jackson's hair catches the dim light from the kitchen, making the scene almost ethereal. I can't see either of their eyes, but I don't need to. I know Jeffery's eyes are as blue as his father's, but his are the innocent blue of the sky, whereas Jackson's change hues along with his mood. Corporate steel. Arctic ice. Caribbean heat.

I need all facets of the man right now. His cool reason to tell me that I'm going to be fine today. His passionate heat so that I can share his strength and believe it.

I shift a bit, suddenly impatient.

I'm certain I made no sound, and yet it doesn't matter. He looks up and sees me, and I watch as his smile erases the lines of exhaustion from his face.

I start to move toward him, but he shakes his head, the movement so small I almost miss it. He glances down, and I realize that Jeffery has fallen asleep. Gently, my husband tugs the bottle out of his little hands and puts it on the table. Then he lifts a finger to his lips, and I nod in understanding.

He stands, the baby against his shoulder, then moves toward me as he rubs Jeffery's back. His smile is both sensual and mischievous, and he cocks his head, signaling for me to follow as he goes back up the stairs.

I do, then stand by his side as he returns Jeffery to his crib. The baby stretches, his little hands curling into fists as his feet kick out, stretching the material of his Winnie-the-Pooh footie pajamas. He makes a snuffling noise, and for a moment, I think he might wake. Then his thumb finds his mouth and he settles, content and safe and loved.

Jackson reaches for my hand, and we walk quietly out of the room. When we reach the hall, he takes one last look, closes the door, and then pulls me roughly to him.

"You're here," I whisper, the complex depth of my happiness and relief camouflaged by the simplicity of my words. "Why are you here?"

"Oh, baby," he murmurs, pulling me into his arms. "You need me. Where else would I possibly be?"

Chapter 2

JACKSON PRESSED A KISS to the top of Sylvia's head as she clung to him. He'd seen how stiff she was on the stairs, and he pulled her closer, as if that could draw out her tension. As if a hug and a kiss could erase the fact that he'd been a goddamned bone-headed idiot.

He should never have gone. What the hell had he been thinking?

Stark Vacation Properties had hired his company, Steele Development, to design and implement the renovation of an old casino hotel on the outskirts of Las Vegas, in an area ripe for economic growth. There'd been trouble on the job yesterday, a combination of site and government issues that added up to the kind of clusterfuck that needed to be nipped in the bud quickly and efficiently, especially considering the bad press that might be generated if word got out about trouble at a Stark or Steele development site.

Sylvia knew that, of course. Though she wasn't assigned to the Vegas project, she worked as a project manager for Stark Real Estate Development. So she'd understood the score and had not only urged Jackson to go, but had demanded it. His associate, Chester Harper, who went by Chess, was both intelligent and a talented architect, but he was also newly licensed and a little too green.

So yes, Jackson had gone. And, yes, he'd dealt with it. Hour after hour with no break, working well into the night so that he could finish what needed to be done and get back to what was most important to him.

But he should never have left in the first place.

"I know what you're thinking," she whispered as she eased away from him, then tilted her head back to look at him. "And don't. I'm fine." She wore no makeup and her short brown hair was tousled from sleep. Her lips parted as if she had something else to say, and it took all of his effort not to press her back against the wall and crush his mouth against hers in a silent, desperate apology.

He didn't. He couldn't. Because though her lips remained silent, her eyes held him at bay. Those bright, whiskey-colored eyes that demanded his attention. That told him without words that she didn't blame him for going no matter how much he blamed himself.

But he also saw pain and a longing so intense it humbled him. Maybe she didn't blame him, but she damn sure needed him. "I shouldn't have gone," he growled, even though they both knew the words were a lie. "I didn't have to be there."

"Of course you did. And now you're back." Her words were simple, but her expression reflected a joyous relief. After a moment, her brow furrowed. "Actually, how did you get back? There aren't any commercial flights this early, and Grayson's not scheduled to return to Vegas to bring you back until noon," she added, referring to the Stark International pilot who'd flown him and Chess to

Vegas yesterday.

"I rented a car and drove."

"Drove! It's five hours." She gaped at him. "Jackson, you drove all night? After working all day and getting next to no sleep the night before?"

"I'd have done more than that in order to get back to you." He cupped her face. "Don't you know that?"

Her eyes said "yes." But her voice said, "Why?"

He didn't answer. Instead, he let his eyes drift over her. Taking in the sweet curves of her body. The silk nightgown that hit mid-thigh. He wanted to take his free hand and trail his finger along the hemline and watch her shiver. Then he wanted to ease his fingertip up until he stroked her breast and teased her nipple, now hard against the material. He wanted to strip the gown off of her and feast upon her. Touching and teasing. Listening to her soft noises, watching as she submitted to pleasure, knowing that she was his.

Already she seemed softer than she had when he'd first seen her on the stairs, as if tension were a physical thing that had been drained from her body, leaving her light and free. He'd put it there by leaving, even though it had been a necessity. And his return had erased it, lightening her burden as he knew it would do.

Now he wanted to go the next step. To free her completely—even if only for a few precious moments—from fear and worry, nightmares and regrets. And not only because he knew she needed it, but because he needed it, too. Needed to feel her against him, to see her open to him. He needed to be certain she was okay. That he hadn't completely fucked this up.

Instead of answering, he led her into the master bedroom. He saw Ronnie sleeping in the chair, and a smile touched his lips, even as he changed his trajectory. He veered away from the bed and crossed to the balcony door. He quickly opened the childproof latch, then led Syl outside and down the spiral staircase to the rooftop patio he'd designed especially for her.

The moment they reached the landing, he drew her roughly to him, taking her by the wrist and bending her arm behind her so that she had no choice but to stand still and listen. "You asked me why I hurried back? Why I drove?" He tightened his grip, and she gasped as the position forced her even closer, the soft noise making his cock twitch. "Why do you think?"

"Tell me."

He bit back a smile. He heard the challenge in her voice along with her rising excitement. "Because you need me, need this," he said, releasing her wrist and cupping her ass. The shock of her bare skin against his palm shot through him, and damned if he didn't almost lose it right then.

She whimpered a little as he tightened his grip on her rear. And then, wanting to torment them both, he urged her even closer so his erection pressed against her belly, and he had to fight the urge to pull her to the ground and take her hard right then. Lord knew they could both use it. Him, taking control. Her, surrendering it.

How many times had they done that very thing? Fought each other's battles? Eased each other's demons? She was like a balm to him, the only thing sometimes that kept him from beating the shit out of whatever poor soul stepped into the ring, an unknowing proxy for all the demons in his life.

And he did the same for her, easing her pain by taking the control she surrendered to him, in marked contrast to the times in her youth when that control had been ripped away without her consent.

They eased each other, helped each other, loved each other. He knew the cause of every hesitation, the color of every fear.

And that was why, when she tilted her head back and he saw the shadow in her eyes, he was certain he knew what was troubling her.

What he didn't know was if Syl herself truly understood.

And so he waited, hating that his wife was in pain, but knowing that even though he was standing right by her, some of the distance she had to walk on her own.

"Syl," he said gently. "What is it?"

"I do want you," she whispered. "God, Jackson. I want you all the time. You know that. But now? Like this? I—I don't want to *need* it so much."

Her voice broke a little, and the sound was like a stab through his heart. He wanted to pull her close and take away all her pain, but he also knew that he had to let her finish talking. So he stayed perfectly still, even though the effort was almost more than he could bear.

"I should be past this. I'm so much stronger now." She dropped her gaze along with her voice. "At least, I thought I was. I shouldn't need your help to fight my battles."

"Oh, baby, you are strong. You're strong and fierce and amazing. But your father is getting out of prison today. Of course you're off kilter."

She managed a wry smile. "That's one way of putting

it."

He pressed on, keeping his voice low. Steady. His eyes stayed on her face, making certain he didn't push too far. "There's nothing wrong with needing my support."

She nodded. "I know. I do. And that's not even all of it. I'm just—I don't know…"

She drifted off, and he cupped her chin, easing it up so that she was forced to look right at him. "Yes, you do," he said firmly. "And so do I."

Her eyes glistened as she blinked back tears. "Do you?"

"Oh, baby, of course. He's on your mind. Feelings. Memories. You think about what he did. How he went out and killed the son-of-a-bitch who abused you. Who stole your virginity and your childhood and your confidence. Do you think I don't realize that you feel like you're obligated to forgive your father for the past simply because he erased that piece of trash?"

She gasped again, but this time it wasn't the sound of desire.

"He killed Reed, baby. He did. And for that we're both grateful, because Robert Cabot Reed was human garbage who would happily have destroyed us both, and was using those vile pictures he took of you as a blunt instrument against the two of us. Your father ended that. But it didn't erase the past."

She looked up at him, her brow furrowed.

"We both know what you need right now. To give yourself over. To surrender control willingly, so you can lose yourself and know that I will always be here to lead you back.

"Jackson—" Her voice broke on a soft little sob.

"You need me," he continued, sliding his hand lower between her legs. "You need me to touch you," he said, his fingertip teasing her slick, wet core. "To take you. To battle back the monsters that I know still haunt your dreams. You need it, and so do I. And that doesn't make either one of us weak. It makes us honest."

As he spoke, he released her, turning her around so that she was facing the glass barrier at the edge of the rooftop. "Hands up," he ordered, not certain if she would comply or pull away because she was still afraid that she would be acting out of weakness. But then she lifted her arms over her head, and that easy, trusting compliance both excited and humbled him.

Slowly, he pulled the nightgown over her body, letting the material glide slowly over her bare skin in a sensual tease. When it was free of her, he tossed it aside, letting it flutter to the wooden decking while she stood naked, the ocean in the distance and their yard spread out before them.

"What about Stella…?" she whispered as he put her hands on the top edge of the barrier, then nudged her legs apart with his knee.

"Shhh." She was referring to their nanny and housekeeper who lived in a bungalow that Jackson had built on the property. He'd designed it deliberately, so that its windows faced only the ocean and the property to the south, thus giving the family privacy in the main house unless Stella happened to be out in the yard.

She wasn't there now, and because Syl had taken the day off from work, he knew that she wasn't scheduled to come to the house for work until ten.

"No talking," he said, more firmly. "You do as I say, or you pay the consequences. Do you understand?"

"Yes, sir." Her voice came out breathy, so full of longing it made him ache.

"Good girl."

He let his eyes rake over her naked form. Her lush curves. The smooth skin of her back and hips. His gaze lingered on the tattoo between her shoulder blades. The one she'd told him she'd gotten after the horror with Reed had finally ended. His gut clenched, and he bent to kiss it, his lips on her skin the only physical connection between them.

"Jackson—"

"Shh. No talking. Not unless I tell you to. Understand?"

She nodded, and his lips curved into a smile as he dropped to his knees, then brushed a kiss over the intricately inked J intertwined with an S. Jackson and Sylvia.

When she'd gotten it, they'd been apart, and she'd believed they'd never get together again. The tattoo was a symbol, a reminder. All of her tats were. A map of pain and triumph. And it felt right to gently kiss each of them now, when the memory of her most tangible pain was pressing so hard against her.

"Turn around," he ordered as he stood, then gently kissed his way around her body. He felt the way her skin tightened and heard the uneven draw of her breath. It was as if she were a mirror of his own desire, and he was *that* close to losing it.

His body tightened, demanding release. He was driving them both crazy by these insubstantial touches when they craved intensity. By gentleness when they wanted it rough.

He spun her back around without a word, and her moan of surprise and anticipation told him it was time. Besides, he was so painfully hard now that he couldn't wait another damn minute. "Bend forward," he ordered, though he was already pressing his hand on her back to force her to comply.

She did, then held onto the edge of the barrier for balance. "Good girl," he said, unbuttoning his jeans and lowering his fly to free his cock. He moved his hand from her back to her hip, holding her still as he inched forward so that his erection nestled tight against her ass. He leaned over her, his chest against her back, his other hand cupping her breast. He brushed his lips over her hair, breathing in the scent of her.

They were so close he could hardly tell where he ended and she began. Her skin was hot to the touch, her breathing coming faster and faster.

Christ, he wanted her, and her response to him—so sensual, so open, so full of need and trust—both humbled him and turned him on even more now than it had before they were married. Now, their connection was complete. Now, she was truly his.

Now, he couldn't wait another moment.

But he had to. Because this morning was about her. What she wanted. What she needed. And so he slid his hand down from her breast to her belly, then lower still until his fingers found her core. Hot and so incredibly wet. And when she squirmed in silent, wanton demand, it took every ounce of restraint not to thrust his fingers inside her.

For that matter, it took all his strength not to hold her

tight, take her hard, and fuck her wildly, brutally.

But he still clung to some remnant of sanity, and he paused, his hand cupping her gently as she squirmed against him, so clearly wanting more. He turned his head, so his lips grazed the back of her ear. “Tell me what you want, baby. I want to hear you say it.”

“You,” she said, the passion in her voice both filling and humbling him. “All I’ve ever wanted is you.”

Chapter 3

YOU.

My word floats away, as if the wind is carrying the truth of it to the world. Because it *is* true. I could live without so many things. But to truly survive, it is Jackson that I need.

I sigh and tighten my hands on the balcony in order to force myself to obey and stay still the way he wants me to. But I'm going to break the rules soon, because I'm almost ready to snap. I'm desperate for his touch, wild with anticipation. And any moment I'm going to break out of the cage of his arms, whirl around, and demand that he fuck me.

He chuckles, the vibrations rolling through me, and I realize he knows exactly what I'm thinking. "Patience," he murmurs as his hand strokes my sex in slow, rhythmic motions. I shift, spreading my legs apart, silently demanding that he touch me. Fill me.

Instead, the bastard slides his hand free, then moves it slowly up my body until he is cupping my breast again. He pinches my nipple, taking me to that point where pain slips gloriously into pleasure. I close my eyes, letting myself enjoy this new assault on my senses. But with Jackson there is always more, and he shifts position so that his steel-hard erection that had been nestled against my ass now slips between my legs, his shaft stroking me from ass to clit as he thrusts again and again.

"Legs together," he demands. "Arch up."

I comply eagerly, and he thrusts harder, one hand kneading my breast as the other moves up from my hip to hold my neck, his thumb and forefinger tight against my jaw. It's an incredibly intimate position, one of absolute control, and I surrender completely, losing myself in the trust I have in this man and the pleasure with which he is battering my body.

"Tell me you like this," he demands, as his fingers tighten on my nipple, as his cock pounds roughly between my legs, stroking and teasing. Never quite taking me far enough, but leaving me in a perpetual state of aroused anticipation.

"I do."

"Tell me you need it."

"Yes, yes. You know I do."

He bends his mouth to my ear, then tugs my lobe with his teeth. "Tell me why."

As he speaks, the hand on my breast snakes down, and he thrusts his fingers inside me even as his cock continues to stroke me intimately. Immediately, my body clenches around him, wanting this, yes. But wanting more. So damn much more.

"Tell me," he repeats, thrusting his fingers further inside me, the deep command in his voice reverberating through me, taking me all the way to the precipice and leaving me teetering on the edge.

"Because I need to surrender." My voice is little more than breath. "To give myself to you completely."

"That's right, baby. But why?"

"Because—" I cut myself off, the words so hard to form. "Because I'm scared," I finally blurt out. "Afraid that when they unlock the jail door they'll also unlock all the memories. All the pain. That the nightmares are going to start all over again."

"And you're afraid I won't be there when you need me?"

"No! Oh, Jackson, no. I just—I just want you now. Now while everything is still okay, as a defense against what might be coming."

He brushes a kiss over the top of my head, and that soft connection soothes me in a different way. "No matter what comes, we'll face it together."

"I know," I say, because if nothing else, I am always certain that Jackson is with me.

"Good girl," he says, and I think I hear a hint of a tease in his voice. "And what do you want as your reward?"

"Please," I beg. "I want you inside me. I want you to fuck me."

"Such demands," he says, and this time I'm sure he's teasing. "And here I thought I was the one in charge."

I'm about to respond that I have no shame, no will. Nothing left in me except desire and that he can have me anyway he wants, if only he will have me. But he doesn't give me the chance. It doesn't matter, anyway. He already knows it. Hell, he's known it from the first moment we met.

Now, he pulls back, then turns me around to face him, the motion so quick it leaves me breathless. I'm still dizzy with lust when he grips my waist, then lifts me so that my ass is on the polished top edge of our glass patio barrier.

I swallow, suddenly aware that I'm naked and balanced precariously above a flagstone patio, and that if I fall it really won't be pretty.

Except Jackson would never let me fall, and so I force myself to relax in his embrace. "Sweetheart," he murmurs, and I hear the understanding in his voice—the knowledge that I surrendered to him even before he asked. That where Jackson is concerned, he can—quite literally—take me to the edge.

He holds me firmly, one arm around my waist and the other at my shoulder. His body is between my legs, and when he tells me to spread my legs and lean back, I hesitate only a second before complying. And as I do, he steps closer, his cock at my core, teasing me but not yet entering. "Legs around me, baby," he says, and the moment I comply, he enters me, thrusting hard as I tighten my legs, both to keep me anchored and because I want to feel each thrust as tight and as deep as possible.

He is filling me completely, his rhythmic thrusts building into a marvelous crescendo that promises a spectacular release. I'm on the edge, leaning back, held aloft only by Jackson's grip. And as my body quivers with the electricity of his touch, infinity spreads out in front around me. The world is at my back, the sky above me, and the sound of the distant ocean all around me.

I'm flying above the castle that Jackson built for me.

I'm loved.

I'm home.

I explode in his arms and feel him do the same. And when his cry of, "I love you baby," washes over me, I know that no matter what demons still haunt me, my life in the moment is perfect.

He eases me back up, and I cling limply to him, making soft sounds of satisfaction.

"You were right to go to Vegas," I murmur as he pulls me back and I wrap my arms around his neck as his strong arms hold me steady. His fingertips lightly stroke my back. "But I'm so, so glad you came back."

"Me too, baby." His voice is as gentle as his soft caress. He lifts me easily, then carries me to the oversized lounge chair that used to be on the back patio of my Santa Monica condo. I have a tenant there now, but I kept the chaise. How could I give it up when it held so many sweet—and bittersweet—memories?

He stretches out, and I curl up beside him. I don't know when he managed it, but he's put the baby monitor on the table in front of us, and I can hear Jeffery starting to stir. Ronnie, I know, will sleep until eight if we let her. But if by chance she wakes up without us, she'll come and find us here.

I think about both of them. Ronnie, curled up with Fred watching out for her. Jeffery, safe and warm in his crib. I feel the same way after Jackson's tending. But even now, with the feel of him still lingering inside me, pinpricks of worry start to needle me, and I shift closer to Jackson, seeking the comfort of his strength.

He bends to kiss my forehead. "Tell me," he demands gently, and I can't help but smile; of course he caught my shift in mood.

"It's nothing," I say. "Not really. I just can't shake the feeling that Reed's still haunting us."

I feel more than hear Jackson's sigh. "Reed's ghost will always try to haunt us. But we know how to vanquish ghosts, Sylvia."

"Yes, I know." I frown, not sure how to put my chaotic thoughts into words. "But it's not ghosts I'm afraid of. Not really. I guess—I mean, it's just that I don't know that my father really ended anything. It's just a salve, a balm. And someday those damn photos are going to turn up again."

I shudder. The day I visited my father in prison, I told him he had to tell the police about the pictures because maybe they would help with his defense. At the very least, their existence might go to a plea of temporary insanity. He refused, though. And the truth is that I'm so damn grateful he did. Because I don't want anyone to see those photos. Even one detective is too much, and if they were released to the public, I don't think I could survive it. I don't want the photos released. Hell, I don't want them to even exist in the universe.

I remind Jackson of that as I lean against him, safe and content. "I feel as though I somehow tempted fate when I told him I could handle it. And now those pictures are going to leap out when we least expect it."

"If they do, we'll fight them. We're strong. And we've already survived hell once." He twists around to look at me more directly, his face full of confident certainty. "What can't we handle if we're together?"

I let his words sink in, hoping that he's right. Then I

snuggle against him, my cheek to his chest, just breathing in the scent of him.

He's right. We can handle it.

But even so …

What I really want is for there to be no potential crisis to handle. But I know that isn't possible. The facts and the photos exist. More than that, they have power over me. And no one can ever change that.

Not even Jackson.

Chapter 4

"SYLVIA? ARE YOU OKAY?"

I've been standing on the patio staring at, but not really seeing, the three bottles of Pinot Noir on the table in front of me. Now I blink, forcing my thoughts back to the present as I turn to look into Stella's dark brown eyes. "What? Sorry. No, I'm fine. Just wondering how many bottles of wine we'll need."

She smiles, but it doesn't quite reach her eyes, and I know I'm not fooling her. Stella had taken care of both the house and Ronnie during the years that Ronnie lived with her great-grandparents. When Ronnie came to live with me and Jackson, Stella had stayed behind in New Mexico. But after Jeffery was born, she'd phoned to ask if we needed a nanny. She missed Ronnie, she'd said, and would love to help with the baby.

We'd said yes immediately and never looked back. She's in her mid-forties, a woman who got pregnant at fifteen and dropped out of high school, then took whatever work she could in order to raise her daughter, now thirty, as a single mom. She's caring and efficient and she adores both the kids, not to mention Fred. And though it took a full four months, Jackson and I finally convinced her to call us by our first names.

Now, she looks around at the wine, spirits, and food piled high onto the long table we've set up on the patio for a casual, buffet-style meal. "I wouldn't worry about the wine," she says gently. "Everything's going to be just fine."

"Thanks." I smile, understanding that she's not really talking about the food, but about the situation. My father, a confessed murderer, returning home.

As far as she and the general public knows, Douglas Brooks killed movie director Robert Cabot Reed in order to stop the movie he intended to make about the Fletcher house—a house that Jackson designed and built, and which became the center of a murder-suicide. A movie that would have pried into the personal details of not only Jackson's life, but Ronnie's, because it was her birthmother who pulled the trigger.

When my father confessed to killing Reed, he told the court that he did it to protect Jackson, the man his daughter loved. But that reason was fabricated. He killed Reed as retribution for me. To erase from the earth the man who had abused me as a child—and who, over a decade later, was using those horrible photos to blackmail me and Jackson into allowing the movie to be made.

Stella has no way of knowing the true motive behind the murder. But I'm certain she knows that there is a history between my father and me, and that whatever else today is, it's not an entirely joyful reunion.

"Everyone will be here soon," she says. "I'm going to go get the smaller plates for dessert."

"That would be great."

She heads off for the kitchen and I continue to stand there feeling uncomfortably nervous and at loose ends.

I draw a deep breath, telling myself I'm being foolish. I'm dreading the moment my dad walks through that door. And at the same time, I wish they'd hurry up and get here so that we can get this over with.

My father was scheduled to be released from Lompac prison at three in the afternoon. Originally, my mother and brother were supposed to pick him up and bring him here for some quiet family time with me, Jackson, and the kids. As it's a two-hour drive, the plan was that they'd arrive around five, we'd have a casual dinner and talk, and then they'd drive the rest of the way to my parents' home in San Diego so that my father could spend his first night of freedom in his own bed.

But the more that plan gelled, the more nervous I'd become. And so I'd ended up inviting Damien, Jackson's half-brother, and his wife Nikki on the pretense that they were family, too. Then I added Cass, my best friend, because she's as close as a sister. Then I added Wyatt Royce to the roster, a good friend who is a professional photographer, saying I wanted candid photos of my kids meeting their grandfather for the first time.

I told myself that Dad would want to be surrounded by people who are living their own lives with absolutely no interest in jumping him in the shower or sticking a shiv between his ribs. In truth, I wanted to make sure I had a crowd to get lost in. Jackson saw the truth, of course, and stopped me before my nerves had me inviting each and every one of my co-workers at Stark Real Estate Development.

Now those nerves are kicking into high gear again and a wave of longing for Jackson washes over me. I sigh, wishing that he were beside me instead of in the nursery, where he'd gone to check on Jeffery.

Reflexively I turn toward the stairs, then smile when I realize that he's back already, just a few yards away in the kitchen. I watch as Stella puts a pile of plates in his arms. He's dressed casually in jeans and a pale blue henley, but neither his casual attire nor the fact that he's carrying dishes lessens the power that he projects. He is confidence and control, and he commands the room simply by being in it.

When he reaches me, he smiles, and I can't help but smile back, my nerves calming simply by virtue of his presence.

"Jeffery?" I ask him, as Stella starts to climb the stairs.

"Just waking up. Stella's going to get him changed and dressed." He cocks his head in the direction of the front door. "They'll be here any minute. I saw Ethan's car turn onto the street from the nursery window."

"Oh." That sense of calm I'd been enjoying disappears in a flash, as if chased away by a swarm of crazed butterflies. "But Cass and Ronnie aren't back yet." I'd sent them to Ralph's, the nearest grocery store, to get slice and bake cookies since Ronnie wanted to "bake" with her grandfather. I'd hoped they'd be back by the time my dad arrived, but the rising panic I hear in my voice is disproportionate to the crisis.

"Hey," Jackson says, putting down the stack of dishes so that he can take my hands. "Everything is going fine."

"I know. I do." My shoulders rise and fall as I take a deep breath. "I'm just…" I trail off with a shrug.

"Nervous? Why wouldn't you be? But, baby, all he cares about right now is that he's free and that he finally gets to hug his grandchildren. That, and what you think of him."

I don't mean to, but I grimace, remembering something else I'd said to my father after he confessed. I told him I wasn't sure I could forgive him, but that I wanted to try. Now he's coming to my home expecting things to be better. As if his jail time had been a line in the sand and now that he's crossed it, everything is sweetness and light, hugs and puppies.

Except it isn't. It really isn't.

"I know," Jackson says simply, obviously understanding my unspoken thoughts as he so often does. "Just tell him the truth, baby."

"The truth?" My voice rises as if in irritation, but is in fact nerves bordering on hysteria. "That I'm still not sure if I love or hate him? That I love what he did for me even though a man is dead because of it. That I want to forgive, but that I'm having a hell of a time letting myself, because isn't that like saying that what he let Cabot do to me doesn't matter anymore? Is that the truth you mean?"

"Yes," he says simply. And then, as I gape at him, he raises my fingers to his lips and kisses them. "Sweetheart, that's exactly what I mean. Your father made a deal with the devil and you were the currency. Maybe it's time to forgive him, or maybe it isn't. Only you know that. But you don't owe him a thing, because killing Reed didn't magically balance the scales."

He draws a breath, and I watch as he forces his body to relax. "But he already knows all of that. He knows the truth. He knows what he did. So whatever the truth is—whatever you now feel about him and however you want to deal with him—that's what you have to tell him. The truth." He caresses my cheek, then meets my eyes, sharing his strength. "It's what you both should expect," he says. "And it's what you both deserve."

"Oh," I say, as the doorbell chimes and my stomach does another backflip. I draw in a deep breath. "I love you, you know."

"I do." He grins. "And I love you."

I nod, letting the purity of those words soak through me. Because when you get right down to it, today and every day, that's all that really matters. "Okay," I say, tightening my fingers around his. "Let's go."

We go together to the door, and I straighten my posture before reaching for the handle. I'm not particularly tall and that rarely bothers me. But sometimes I want all the ammunition I can get to feel stronger and more confident, and right then a few extra inches would have made me happy. Too bad we were doing this casual. Otherwise, I could have worn stilettos.

I flash a quick practice smile, then open the door to reveal Ethan and my father. Ethan rushes forward, wrapping me in a tight hug. "Missed you, Silly," my brother says, and I grin happily at the ridiculous nickname.

"You saw me last week," I remind him, laughing.

"Fair enough," he says as he pulls back and moves to shake Jackson's hand. "The truth is I miss my niece and nephew. Oh! There he is," he says, looking over Jackson's shoulder at Stella, who has entered the foyer with Jeffery.

Ethan claps Jackson on the shoulder, then bolts past him to gather up the baby, leaving my father lingering on the threshold.

"Douglas," Jackson say, extending his hand. "It's so good to see you. Come on in."

He enters slowly, and I can't help but notice how much more frail and unsteady he seems, as if he's aged disproportionately to the years. He pauses in front of me, and his arms move forward to hug me, but then he hesitates and pulls them back, obviously unsure. I step up, then wrap my arms awkwardly around him. "I'm really glad you're here, Daddy," I say, my voice tinny with emotion.

I release him and step back, grateful when Jackson's arm goes around my shoulder.

In front of me, my father shifts his weight from foot to foot. "Me too."

With a start, I realize that my mother isn't here. "Didn't Mom come?"

"Yeah, well…" He swallows. "She told Ethan she just wanted to see me at home." His expression is as gentle as I've ever seen it when he adds, "Don't blame her. I think she's emotionally exhausted."

I nod, because the tightness in my chest prevents actual speech. Jackson squeezes my shoulders in silent, stalwart support. It's such a little thing, but I'm so damn grateful. If nothing else, Jackson makes me feel loved.

The truth is, I don't know why I expected she'd come. My guess is that she backed out once Ethan told her about the celebration at my house. Because ever since Ethan got sick—ever since Daddy raised the money for his treatment by hiring me out to Reed on the pretense of being a studio model for his photographs—my mother has treated me as a non-entity.

Nice to know some things never change.

The silence hangs awkwardly between us. After a moment, my dad glances around. "Looks like you and Jackson have built a nice life."

Perhaps it's my imagination, but I think I hear hope in his voice. Like maybe the fact that I have a beautiful home and an amazing husband and wonderful children exonerates him.

I feel myself tense, and I hear Jackson's voice in my head telling me to just tell him the truth.

I know I should—in fact, I'm searching for the words to do just that—when I hear a car door slam behind us and then the patter of little feet on the walkway. "Grandpa!"

My father's face changes in a heartbeat. All hesitation gone. Worry erased. Fear extinguished. There's nothing but joy now.

Even his body seems lighter, and he bends down with a grace he hadn't displayed when he'd entered the house just a few moments before.

Ronnie races past me into the house as Cass's voice drifts in after her, her tone ironic as she says, "We're back."

"Cookies, Grandpa!" Ronnie says, brandishing a tube of slice and bake chocolate chip cookies. "I'm gonna make 'em for you! Wanna watch? Please, please, pretty please?"

"Can't think of anything I'd rather do," he says, looking at her with the utmost sincerity. He enfolds her free hand in his. "Lead the way," he says as he winks at me.

My heart does a little flip-flop, and I watch as they head toward the kitchen, Ronnie skipping happily and chattering nonstop.

And I think that maybe—just maybe—this will all turn out okay.

Chapter 5

BY SIX O'CLOCK, everyone has arrived, the sun has set, and our backyard looks like a fairy playground, illuminated by dozens of cleverly placed strings of light. Of all the guests, Jeffery is the only one who has faded. In contrast, Ronnie is twirling in the backyard, showing off for her grandfather in the sparkling lights as Wyatt moves around them with a confident grace. He's in his element, taking candid shots that I'm certain will be hanging on our walls within the week.

I'm in a rocker, moving slowly back and forth, knowing I should go put him in his crib, but I'm too comfortable, and so I content myself by watching Jackson.

He's by the bar with Ethan and Damien, his half-brother. All three of their heads are bent over, and Jackson is sketching something on a cocktail napkin, scratching things out and revising as the other two men comment. I have no idea what they're working on, but I'm struck once again by the striking similarity between Jackson and Damien. The dark hair. The chiseled faces. But mostly it's an attitude. Confidence. Power. Razor-focused ambition.

I'm watching them when Nikki drops into a chair beside me. A former model, she's stunning in a girl-next-door kind of way, and her smile is wide and genuine. She nods toward the men. "My bet's on the moon."

I cock my head, clueless. "The moon?"

"They both have that look. And I don't know Ethan that well yet, but he's looking pretty intense as well. I figure they're up to something. And since between Damien and Jackson, they've pretty much conquered the planet, I'm thinking the moon is their next frontier."

I laugh. "You might have a point. You've got to admit, if Jackson builds a house up there, it would have one hell of a view."

"Jackson's building another house?" Cass asks as she approaches, a glass of wine in one hand and a highball of whiskey in the other. Her hair is purple today, the vibrant hue matching the tail feathers of the exotic bird tattoo that graces her shoulder.

Nikki and I look at each other and grin. "When isn't he?" I ask.

"Good point." She holds out each glass in turn. "Wine or scotch?"

"Scotch," I say. I stopped nursing a few months ago, and while I loved bonding with my son that way, I confess that I'm happy to add alcohol back into my food and drink repertoire.

"You got it." She passes the glass to me and raises a brow in inquiry as she turns to Nikki.

"I'm good," Nikki says, holding up her own glass of red.

"Excellent." Cass takes a long swallow of the wine. "More for me." She looks around, then hustles over to one of the patio chairs and drags it back to us. She sits down, takes another swallow, and grins. "So what are we talking about?"

"Nothing juicy," Nikki says, her mouth quirking ironically. "Guess we're just boring married women. Better watch out, Cass. You'll be joining our ranks soon enough."

Cass and her girlfriend officially got engaged about seven months ago, but so far they haven't set a date for the wedding. Cass tells me it's just because they're both so focused on clearing a path through their crazy-busy work lives, but for the first time in our long friendship, I'm afraid she's not telling me something.

Cass snorts in response to Nikki's assessment. "One," she says holding up a finger, "I'm never boring."

I nod. "The lady has a point."

"Two, I know both of you, remember? Not a whole lot of boring going on there either. And three," she adds, with a wicked grin, "I may not go for the half of our species who sport the Y chromosome, but that doesn't mean I can't assess the value of the merchandise. And ladies? Neither one of you ended up in Dullsville."

Nikki's musical laughter fills the area, and Damien looks up at her and smiles with such adoration and affection that I can't help but sigh. I've seen that same look in Jackson's eyes more times than I can count, and it always melts me.

"What's that look for?" Cass demands.

I shrug innocently. "Just thinking about family resemblances."

Beyond our circle, I see my dad and Ronnie heading inside, probably for more cookies. Wyatt doesn't follow.

Instead, he walks a slow circle around the patio, his camera clicking as he photographs the men and then aims the lens toward us.

I look at Cass, trying not to pay attention to Wyatt. I'm the one who asked him to take candids, after all. "Where's Siobhan tonight?"

"Working." She makes a face. "This new job is a killer, and she hates it, but so far she hasn't found anything better."

"I remember those days," Nikki says. "Tell her good luck."

"Will do. She'd like to do what we're doing—run her own business. But she's not ready to make the leap. I've told her she can be the marketing director at Totally Tattoo," Cass adds, referring to the tattoo parlor she owns, "but I think she's nervous about working together. Oh!" she adds, "guess who I saw yesterday when I was having lunch. You'll never guess."

I roll my eyes. "In that case, just tell me." Jeffery stirs in my arms. I bend over and kiss his forehead, and out of the corner of my eye, notice that Wyatt has snapped a photo.

"Mila Sanchez."

My brows rise; she's right, I never would have guessed. "No kidding? Where?"

"I was over at Blacklist," she says, referencing the funky bar that's just two doors down from her shop.

"Did she recognize you?"

"I'm not certain, but I think so. She didn't say anything, but she got this pinched look on her face, like she was holding back something really nasty she wanted to say to me. Or maybe she just needed to fart."

I snort, but I have to admit the mental picture is accurate. Whenever Mila got irritated, that was exactly the expression she'd have on her face.

"Wait," Nikki says. "Who is Mila?"

"You never met her?" I guess I shouldn't be surprised. Nikki might be married to Damien, but that doesn't mean she's met all of the thousands of people who work at Stark International. "She was a floater secretary. I had to fire her ages ago. Cass met her a few times at the office and after work happy hours."

"She seemed so normal," Cass adds.

Nikki twirls her hand, urging us to continue. "So? What happened?"

"Gross incompetence coupled with extreme stupidity," I say.

"Oh, please," Cass protests. "Gross incompetence sounds dull. Like forgetting to mail a package. Or putting a call through without screening it. But I'm totally on-board with the extreme stupidity assessment."

Nikki laughs. Wyatt moves in closer, his expression one of intense concentration. I figure he's trying to get a better shot of her very camera-friendly face.

"Well, don't just leave me hanging," Nikki says, when neither Cass nor I jump in to fill the conversational gap. "What did she do?"

"Hit on Jackson," Cass says, in the kind of voice a judge would use to pronounce a death sentence.

"No way!"

"Yeah, well, there's more," I add.

"She hit on Damien, too," Cass blurts. "*And* she insinuated that the three of them were having a thing. Like a three-way."

Nikki clamps her hand to her mouth, obviously in an effort to keep from spewing her wine. "How did I not know this?"

"I think you and Damien were out of the country when it went down. At any rate, good riddance." I shudder. "I haven't seen her in ages. I sincerely hope it stays that way."

Wyatt's back in my field of vision, and he honestly doesn't look too comfortable. I suppose that's a downside of candid photography; you're always overhearing conversations you'd rather not. I flash a smile to let him know it's hardly confidential, but he looks quickly away. Then aims his camera at Ronnie, who's skipping toward Jackson, this time without my father nearby.

I watch as Jackson scoops her effortlessly up and perches her on the edge of the bar so she can be part of the conversation with her two uncles. The motion is so gentle and automatic and loving that I feel my heart squeeze. And when Jackson meets my eyes across the fairy-lit patio, I sigh from the wash of heat and love that bubbles inside me.

"—mansion tomorrow?"

I jerk toward Nikki, realizing I'd zoned out. "Sorry, what?"

"I asked if you were still going to the costume party at the Segel mansion tomorrow."

"Oh, yeah. I think so." She's talking about Anika Segel, the four-time Academy Award winning film icon and one of Hollywood's grand dames. She's invited Jackson and me to her annual charity event because Jackson is designing a second home for her in Costa Rica. "I wish you and Damien were coming, too." They, of course, were invited simply because Damien is Damien.

"So do I," Nikki says. "It sounds like fun. But we'll be in Austin by tomorrow evening. As much as I'm looking forward to the South by Southwest conference, I'm still a little bummed. I mean, even I know who Anika Segel is, and I know next to nothing about Hollywood."

Nikki's company was hired to put together a smart phone adaptation of a popular board game, and they're rolling out the app at Austin's long-standing film, interactive media, and music event. Damien's going mostly to be with his wife, but since the man never stops working, he's also scheduled a few meetings with some tech start ups.

I may not be his assistant anymore, but I haven't broken the habit of keeping an eye on his schedule.

"Well, I'm incredibly jealous," Cass admits. "I think it sounds fabulous."

"Jackson thinks it's silly," I admit. "Not the idea of a charity event, but the costumes. His take is why not just have black tie and be civilized with scotch and martinis?"

"It's a valid question." The deep, sensual voice behind me sends shivers down my spine, and I twist around to see that Jackson has moved away from the bar and circled over to us.

He bends lower so that I feel his breath on my ear as he says, "To be honest, I've had a change of heart. I'm looking forward to it. Immensely."

I swallow as both Cass and Nikki look amused. "Really?"

He presses his hand to the back of my neck, sending a cascade of warmth through my whole body that pools between my legs so that I have to fight not to squirm a little in my chair.

"I've had an attitude adjustment," he admits.

Case's brows lifts, and she glances at Nikki. "I think that's our cue to leave."

"Not at all," Jackson says. "I'm just taking a detour before I go push Ronnie on the swings. But you," he adds as he puts both hands on my shoulders. "You should consider this a promise of things to come. Tomorrow night. Edward will pick you up here at eight. I'll meet you at the party at nine."

"Meet me there?" I'm breathless. "Why?"

"Because we're going to play a game. It's a costume party, right? So I expect you to do it up. If I find you within an hour, I win. Any longer, you win." His grin promises all sorts of wicked delights. "And since I know you so well, baby, it won't be a challenge at all."

I raise my brows. "You've thrown down the gauntlet, mister."

He chuckles, then kisses me. "Let the games begin."

I catch Cass's eyes; she's grinning.

"Wait!" I call after Jackson. He pauses, then turns back to me. "What do I get if I win?"

He lifts a shoulder casually. "Whatever you want."

"And if you win?"

He rakes a heated gaze over me, and my heart skips a beat. "You."

"Oh," I say, my body just a little bit numb. "Then I guess either way, I win."

His mouth twitches, but he doesn't respond. Just holds my eyes for a moment before turning and walking away.

I watch him go, thinking that yeah, I'm going to enjoy

this party.

I'm still basking in the glow when Nikki sighs. "Nice to know that little one hasn't turned down the heat," she says, smiling fondly at Jeffery, still asleep in my arms.

"He really hasn't," I say, and feel a blush rise on my cheeks.

Cass laughs. "Okay, we have to figure out a costume. Tomorrow morning. My place. Ten. We shop."

Since Cass is an expert shopper, particularly in the kinds of used and vintage stores I'll probably have to prowl to find a suitable costume, I readily agree.

"I'm going to leave you to it," Nikki says. "I feel a sudden urge to go find my husband." She winks, then heads out onto the lawn, where Damien has joined Jackson at the swing set.

"I need to put this little guy in his crib. Wanna come up with me?"

"Nah, you go ahead. I'm going to catch up with Ethan. Grab me another wine on your way back?"

I promise I will, then head inside, cradling my son. I'm passing through the kitchen when my father calls my name. I turn, surprised to see him sitting at the small work station in an unlit corner.

"Daddy?"

"I've had a hard time getting close enough to talk to you tonight," he says with a wan smile.

I frown. "I've been here. Sitting mostly. Definitely not hiding."

"No, no." He sighs, then stands. "I just mean it's hard to navigate around the elephant in the room."

My chest tightens. "Oh." I open my mouth, but I'm

not sure what to say. That I'm glad he's out of prison, but not sure that I can forgive him? That I tried, but it just doesn't feel right? That the scars of my childhood have faded, but they're still there, and always will be?

Since I can't figure out where to begin, I just stand there holding the baby, my mouth open like some gasping fish. I feel foolish. And, suddenly, I feel angry. Because he's the man who's made me feel that way.

As if he senses the storm in my head, he lifts his hand. "Wait. There's something I need to say, and I've had about two years to think about how I want to say it." He takes a deep breath. "I don't expect you to forgive me. For that matter, I don't think I want you to."

I open my mouth, not to respond, but in surprise.

He hurries on. "I—I screwed up, honey. I know it. And killing Reed didn't change that, although I'm not ashamed that it makes me feel damn good knowing I rid the world of that vermin. So I don't want to ask you for forgiveness. And I don't want to ask you to forget. But I just want to ask if we can start fresh. From right now. Not erasing the past, but moving on from it." He swallows, looking small and uncertain. "Do you think—do you think we could try that?"

Tears prick my eyes and I blink. In my arms, Jeffery squirms, and I realize I've been holding him tight. "Yeah," I say, as what feels like the weight of the world slips from my shoulders. "I think we can do that. At least, I know I want to try."

Chapter 6

WHEN EDWARD RINGS the bell at eight o'clock the next night, all I can think is that Cass is a genius. Because as I stand and look in the full-length mirror in our bedroom, I can't help but think that I look freaking incredible.

I'd awakened that morning to find her in the kitchen, having let herself in with her spare key.

"I passed Jackson on his way out," she said. "He said to tell you he took the kids to Stella's bungalow. Apparently they're staying there all day and all night, so that—and I quote—you can concentrate on amazing him. And then he told me to tell you that he'd find you tonight. Within his allotted hour," she adds. She grins wickedly. "Part of me thinks we should do up the costume brilliantly. And another part of me thinks you should just make it easy on him." She waggles her brows. "After all, sounds to me like you're going to have a great time losing this particular competition."

She's right about that. After the party last night ended and Jackson and I were in bed, I'd curled up against him, making no secret of the fact that I wasn't too tired to enjoy our newly restored privacy. He asked me how I was doing after seeing my father, and he kept tight attention on my eyes as I told him about the detente with my dad and then assured him that I was doing okay.

Apparently that was the wrong thing to say, because he told me that was good. And then he held me close and proceeded to tell me in explicit, delicious, panty dropping detail exactly what he was *not* going to do with me last night.

"Because I want you desperate tomorrow," he'd explained, when I'd protested. "I want you to spend every moment of Saturday thinking about the way I'm going to touch you. The way I'm going to find you and tear your costume off you when we get home. The way I'm going to steal you away to a dark corner at the party, press one hand over your mouth so you don't make a sound, and then make you shatter in my arms."

He brushed his lips over my ear, and I trembled, on the verge of exploding from nothing more than his tantalizing promise. "And no one in that house full of people will know that the glow on your skin isn't from the party but from passion. Not from the festivities, but from me. And sweetheart? That's only the beginning."

I whimpered. I begged. I slid my hand down his body until my fingers curled around his rock-hard cock. But all he did was push me away, a devious gleam in his eye. "And no touching yourself," he warned. "No cheating, or I might not come to the party at all."

"Bastard," I'd said, then rolled onto my side and pretended to pout.

"I am," he agreed as he spooned against me, but not

before sliding his finger up the back of my thigh, then between my legs, to tease my core just enough to make me crazy—yet not enough to make me come. "Now sleep," he said. "Tomorrow will come faster that way."

Because I'd had no choice, I obeyed, and I'd woken up even more desperate for his touch, his kisses, his cock. But he was already gone, and I couldn't remember the specifics of my dreams.

All I knew was that eight o'clock couldn't come fast enough. And that sometime during the day, I had to put together a costume that was not only the perfect disguise, but would also bring him to his knees.

With Cass at the helm, I managed to do just that.

"The first thing we have to do is change your overall look," she'd said as she circled me, a pencil in her mouth like a cigarette. She carried a notepad and every few moments she'd scribble something, then nod her head and say something like, "Hell, yeah," or, "Oh, he is going to be blown away," while I stood like an idiot wondering what the devil she was plotting.

Turns out we didn't need to go shopping, because Cass brought the world to me. "Stuff I haven't gotten around to altering," she'd said. "Or that I grabbed for Halloween, or just because it was a bargain. And the make-up is from the shop for when we do cover work."

I realized with a start that she'd thought about something I hadn't. Unless I was going to show none of my back, I had to cover my tattoos or Jackson would recognize me right away. Fortunately, Cass also does make-up for actors who need to cover their ink before a shoot or a play. Which means she's an expert at hiding her work.

We tackled that first, and Cass covered every tattoo on my back and my legs, then proceeded to cover the tats on my breasts. "Because I think we want to go risqué," she said. Turned out she had a specific gown in mind, and it was very revealing. The top was form fitting and backless. The skirt was made entirely of overlapping strips of material that shimmied and shimmered, revealing lots of leg as I walked.

The arms and front were made of a fine black lace, with the exception of two triangular shapes that covered my breasts. Or, rather, they covered my breasts and then some, because Cass stuffed the bodice with silicone inserts, taking me all the way up to a D-cup.

"Seriously?" I asked, but she just shrugged.

"The idea is for him not to recognize you. And the hair has got to go."

"My hair?"

"Just temporarily." She reached into the smallest of the three huge duffels she'd dragged to the house this morning, then pulled out a wig. The hair was long and black with a hint of red, and even though the idea of wearing a wig all night sounded less than fun, I couldn't deny that I wanted to see where this makeover took me.

She put it on with some sort of special tape, but promised it would come off easily with alcohol. She didn't let me look at myself, but I had to admit I liked the feel of the strands on my shoulders. I'd always loved my hair when I wore it long, and I'd only cut it because Reed had also liked it.

Maybe it was time to grow it out again and just mentally flip Reed the bird.

I pondered that as she did my make-up, narrating her work as she went through it. Adding a mole, making my lips bigger with liner and color. Adding more depth to my cheekbones. "I thought about getting you an insert for your mouth to make your jaw wider, but figured you'd balk."

"Yeah," I said. "You figured right." Honestly, there was enough going on here that I rather hoped there'd be an award for Best Costume. If so, I would undoubtedly win and the statue could live in Cass's living room.

"One more thing" she finally said, "and then we'll put on the eyelashes and the shoes."

The "one more thing" turned out to be colored contacts that she swore would make my brown eyes turn a vivid green. Then she had me try on three different pairs of shoes until she found four-inch platforms I could actually walk in.

"Damn, I'm good," she said as she dragged me to the mirror right at eight o'clock. And she was right. I looked freaking amazing. More important, I didn't look at all like me. Especially not when I put on the black lace mask that went so perfectly with the dress.

Now, the door chimes again, and I realize I've been so lost in my mental praise of my best friend's transfiguration abilities that I completely spaced out.

"It's time," I say, feeling almost as excited as a girl going on a first date.

We hurry to the front door and Cass opens it, revealing me to Edward, whose eyes go wide. "Amazing," he says. "You look exceptional."

"It's all Cass's handiwork," I say.

"But would you recognize her?" Cass demands.

"No," he says. "But I'm still betting on Jackson."

I laugh. Honestly, it's probably a good bet.

"You did a great job," he tells Cass.

"Hell, yeah, I did," Cass says, then buffs her nails on her chest before giving me a careful hug, so as not to mess up my make-up or my costume.

I leave her behind, then follow Edward to an unfamiliar white limo. I shoot him a quizzical look, and he lifts a shoulder. "Mr. Steele was very precise. Eight o'clock arrival. Nine at the party. An unfamiliar limo—I borrowed this one from a buddy with a car service—and I'm not to open the door for you. He's leaving that to the valet at the party."

"Okay then," I say, but I'm fighting back a smile. Jackson's serious about this game—and if he saw Edward or a Stark limo, he'd see me. And that would take the fun out of the hunt.

It's silly, but I actually feel a little nervous as Edward maneuvers us from the house to Beverly Hills. I feel a bit like a girl going on her first date. Jittery. Unsure. But certain it's going to be a grand adventure.

The Segel mansion is situated on several prime acres in the hills. It's tucked away down a private drive and accessed only through a guarded gate. It was built during Hollywood's golden age by Anika's father, Arthur Segel, a brilliant movie producer and director who also happened to have co-founded the studio behind most of the movies that brought Anika to fame and glory.

She told Jackson that it was her father who insisted she keep the family name when she got married. "He can offer you a lot, sweetheart," he'd said. "But not a better name."

She'd listened, and her fame—and her fortune—had only grown.

I've only met her once, but I found her to be both charming and intimidating. And even now, in her eighties, she's a force of nature.

I'm full of anticipation when Edward brings the limo to a halt and an actual footman opens the door, then offers me a hand to get out. And my eagerness isn't just for Jackson, though that certainly tops the list. But for the party as a whole.

The footman escorts me to the front door, and for a moment I'm afraid he's going to ask for my name and then announce me. But he simply tells me to have a good time, explains about the upcoming silent auction, then nods politely and heads back outside.

By the time I reach the ballroom, I realize there's more in my favor than just the amazing costume Cass put together. This party is a crush. I can barely move, much less find Jackson, and I know his costume won't be as intricate as mine. The odds of him finding me in an hour are seriously skewed in my favor.

Though I'm enjoying the taste of impending victory, I'd rather be enjoying a glass of wine, and so I veer off to my right, skirting the edge of the ballroom as I head to one of the many bars that have been set up. I'm groping in my bag for my drink ticket and not paying attention to where I'm going when I bump hard against someone, then jump as I realize it's Wyatt.

He'd been chatting with a woman dressed like an elven princess, and now he turns to face me, his expression mildly irritated, but then downshifting to polite.

"I'm so sorry," I say. "I wasn't looking where I was going."

His bold smile is wide with a hint of invitation as he looks me up and down, and I'm both amused and a little bit mortified as I remember that while Wyatt doesn't have girlfriend, I've heard enough gossip among my friends and co-workers to know that women are eager to be on his arm. And, presumably, in his bed.

He takes a step toward me, and for the first time I study him critically. Honestly, it's enough to make me believe the gossip. He's exceptionally good looking, with an athletic build and the kind of wind-swept, golden-brown hair that always looks like he's just rolled out of bed. He moves with a confident grace, and when he looks at me with his photographer's eye, it's as if he's seeing all my secrets.

That's an illusion, of course. Because at the moment, my biggest secret is my identity. And considering the sensual twist of his mouth as he starts to speak, it's clear that he hasn't recognized me.

"Wyatt," I whisper, jumping in before he says something that will embarrass us both. "It's me. Sylvia."

He stops, and for just an instant, his expression is confused. Then it shifts to understanding before rounding third and heading on home to mortification.

"Syl—" he begins, but I cut him off, tamping down on the air as if to force a lower volume. It works. "I didn't recognize you," he continues, and despite the whisper, I can clearly hear the apology in his voice.

"That's the idea," I say. "Costume ball, remember?" I can't stop the confident grin that spreads over my face.

After all, if a man with a photographer's eye doesn't see the real me, then maybe I really do have a shot at fooling Jackson.

I take a step toward him, and this time I actually want to look like we're flirting and not old friends. Because Jackson is somewhere in this room, and he's watching everyone. "Are you working this party?" I frown because I don't see his camera.

"No, it's much more servile than that." The corner of his mouth twitches. "This is a command performance. My grandmother insisted I come."

"Oh." I'm still confused. "Who's your grandmother?"

"Anika Segel."

"*Oh.*" How the hell did I not know this? I want to ask him if he's pulling my chain, but before I can figure out how to phrase it, Jamie Archer bounces up to Wyatt. She's decked out as Marilyn Monroe, and she looks incredible. Jamie is Nikki's best friend, and she's drop-dead, camera-friendly, Hollywood gorgeous. I know she tried making it as an actress, but she seems to have settled in with her job as an on-air celebrity reporter.

"Someone over there is looking for you," she says to Wyatt. "A green-eyed cat. Can't miss her."

"Thanks." He nods to me. "See you later, Syl."

Jamie's brows rise. "Sylvia? Damn, girl, you look amazing."

"That's the idea," I say. "I'm so glad you're here. I didn't realize you were coming."

"Got lucky," she said. "The job has a few perks, that's for sure."

"Speaking of celebrity gossip, did you know that Anika

Segel is Wyatt's grandmother?"

"No way!" she says, and I feel a sense of relief that I'm not the only one who is completely clueless.

Jamie's brow furrows. "I think I smell a story."

"Just remember it didn't come from me." I have no idea if I've broken a confidence. Why on earth had Wyatt never mentioned that his family is Hollywood royalty?

It's not a question that bothers me for too long, though, because Evelyn Dodge glides over. Her focus is on Jamie, but she aims a polite smile in my directions. She looks exactly like herself in a flowing evening gown in a violent shade of orange. It's stunning, but it definitely doesn't qualify as a costume.

"Not dressing up?" Jamie asks.

Evelyn chuckles, then lifts a black stick with a mask attached to one end. She puts it over her face and smiles. "All I need," she says. "Why the hell would I want to come to a Hollywood shindig and *not* be recognized?"

She has a point. One of my favorite people, Evelyn Dodge is practically a Hollywood landmark. She's been in the business for years, has held every job imaginable, and has recently returned to agenting. In fact, she represents Jamie.

A high-end Hollywood charity event is probably her happy hunting ground.

She confirms my thinking when she taps Jamie's shoulder with her mask. "You should mingle. Garreth Todd is over by the pool," she says, naming one of Hollywood's brightest stars. "Play your cards right and you can line up an interview." She frowns, looking Jamie's costume up and down. "But take Ryan with you. Todd's an absolute horn dog. Where is Ryan, anyway?"

"Over there," Jamie says, pointing vaguely across the ballroom. Her long-term boyfriend is Stark International's Chief of Security, and so I know him well. She shifts her attention to me. "By the way, where's Jackson?"

At the question, Evelyn's brows rise. "Sylvia?"

"Shhh," I say. "I'm in disguise."

Her mouth twists, clearly amused. "Are you? Hiding from Jackson?"

"Something like that," I admit. "We came separately. Now he has to find me."

"Really?" Jamie's brows are practically to her hairline. "Why?"

"I'll tell you later," I say, realizing that by talking to these particular women, I've probably made it too easy on him. "I'm going to go mingle."

"Date night," Evelyn says in a tone of absolute surety. "They're doing it up right."

"Not yet," I say with a wink. "But we will be."

Chapter 7

THE CLOCK CONTINUES to tick, yet Jackson doesn't find me. I can't decide if I'm thrilled I'm so close to winning, or disappointed that I won't be Jackson's prize.

Of course, I haven't seen him either, which surprises me. I didn't expect him to get deep into costume. And with only fifteen minutes to go on the hour, I start scouring every face at the party.

Most people are recognizable, having gone more with the idea of a costume than an all-out disguise. I see a woman with dark hair by the bar and am just thinking she looks familiar when she turns toward me and I recognize Mila. I consider going and talking to her—after all, it seems like such an odd coincidence to see her so soon after Cass mentioned her—but I hold back. For one, I don't particularly like her. For another, I don't want to have to introduce myself in my fantastical costume.

I'm not terribly surprised she's here, though. I'd heard she'd moved on to work in television. I'd assumed reality TV, but now I wonder if she's not working in scripted drama or on features. After all, she's talking to Lyle Tarpin, a popular television and movie actor whose star is about to explode. He recently play the lead in a movie that my friend Jane wrote. It's coming out in the summer, but the advance buzz says it's going to be a game changer for Tarpin's career.

I continue looking around the room, and make a mental note to tell Cass that her favorite actress and crush, Kirstie Ellen Todd, is here.

I'm toying with the idea of being completely gauche and asking Kirstie for an autograph when I feel warm hands cup my waist.

I stiffen.

"You are by far the most beautiful creature in this room," the deep voice behind me says.

"You should be careful. My husband might be watching."

"Would serve him right if I turned you around and kissed you right now. Hard. Deep. The way you should be kissed." He moves in tight against me, and I feel the press of his erection against my ass. "He must be a fool to leave you alone in that outfit with so many hungry men."

"Maybe he likes to see me as the object of other men's appetites."

My companion chuckles. "I imagine he does. It's nice to know something beautiful you own is coveted by other people. He does own you, doesn't he?" he asks, trailing a fingertip up my spine, and sending a series of little shivers coursing through me.

"Completely."

"Then why isn't he here with you right now?"

I tilt my head to the side, considering the question. "I don't know. Maybe he likes to watch?"

I spin in his arms, then face my husband. He's dressed like the Man in Black from *The Princess Bride*. A black mask over his eyes, a black bandana on his head. And a pair of tight black pants that make my pulse speed up. He looks like sex on a stick, especially with those blue eyes behind the mask, and the beard scruff on his jaw framing that rich, sensual mouth.

I have no idea how I've missed seeing him, but now I drink him in, and like a woman parched, I feel myself coming alive. My body is flushed, my nipples hard. And I'm so very, very wet. "Is that what you want?" I ask. "To watch me with another man?"

It's a tease, of course, and I expect him to laugh it off. I don't expect the heat that flares in his eyes, along with a dangerous, possessive spark. "I've been watching you," he says, glancing quickly to the second floor. "I've been watching you for almost an hour. Did you think I couldn't find you right away? I will always find you, Syl. I know the way you move. The way you smile."

He leans in, so that I feel his breath on my face as he speaks. "I'm so goddamn hard from watching you. But baby, I'd kill any other man who touches you like that. You're mine. And I don't share."

The words shoot through me, arousing me even more than I believed possible.

"Then tell me what you do want," I murmur. "Whatever you want."

He traces his hand down my arm, the brush of his fingertip on the lace that separates his skin from mine shockingly arousing. "I want you to go to the ladies' room," he says, leaning in so that I feel the heat of his breath on my cheek. "I want you to take off your panties. And I want you to bring them to me."

My core clenches, heat rippling through me. My pulse kicks up, my nipples strain against the soft material of the bodice. I'm craving his touch. Hell, I'm desperate for it. And I hold his gaze, then lick my lips before very firmly saying, "No."

Surprise flashes in his eyes, and his left brow lifts above the mask, the scar that bisects it adding a dangerous edge to his heated expression. "No? Is this an act of pure defiance?" he asks, sliding a hand behind my neck and making me gasp again as he roughly tugs me closer. He holds me like that for a moment, then moves his hand down to cup my rear through the thin material of the dress. "Or is it an invitation for me to spank your sweet ass?"

I swallow, then tilt my head to the side. I smile innocently, my eyes wide. "I don't know what you mean, Mr. Steele. I'm not being defiant—I just can't do the impossible."

I continue before he can articulate the question I see forming on his face. "The fact is, I'm not wearing any underwear."

This time, it's his turn to groan, and I know the man well enough that I recognize the sound as one of pure, primal need. I've surprised him. More than that, I've aroused him even more than he already was.

I glance down at his crotch and see his erection straining against the tight black leather. "You really should do something about that," I tease.

"Believe me. I intend to." He takes my hand and pulls me to the side, the sudden movement jarring a surprised gasp out of me.

"Are we leaving?"

"Hell, no," he says, and a wave of disappointment crashes over me. At least until he leads me into the back yard and over to a small copse of trees that is just out of the circle of colored lights that illuminate the pool and the yard beyond.

"What—" I begin, but he presses a finger to my lips, hushing me even as he turns me around so that his other hand is on my waist, and he has me positioned so that my back is nestled up against his chest as he leans against one of the trees.

"Just look," he says. "Just listen. The costumes, the lights. The sounds of laughter. The music from the orchestra. Just watch. Just enjoy. Just *feel*."

On the last, his hand slides up my thigh, moving beneath the long strips of overlapping material that make up the skirt of this dress. It's solid until about two inches below my ass, allowing for modesty even when going commando, but that is no deterrent to Jackson's nimble fingers that are now tracing a path along the line of sensitive skin between my thigh and my sex.

"Don't you remember?" he murmurs in my ear. "I told you I'd take you to a dark corner. I promised to make you shatter. Sweetheart," he adds, taking the hand from my waist and putting it gently over my mouth, "I'm going to make you come so hard you scream."

I want to protest that he's crazy. That we're in public. That anyone can see.

But the truth is that I don't care.

No, that's actually not the truth. The truth is that the

possibility excites me. To be standing here in the dark with Jackson's fingers up my skirt and his hand over my mouth as he teases me into a fever pitch.

I know he's right—it's dark where we are. Secluded. But there's still a chance. Still that danger.

It's enticing. Exciting. And right now I'm drunk enough on lust to want it.

Oh, how I want it.

I want to melt against my husband. I want to submit to his whims.

I want him to make me explode.

And right now, he's doing a damn good job of working toward that goal.

I try to gasp as his fingertip slides over my slick folds to tease my clit, but his hand tightens on my mouth, and I have to suck in air through my nose. At the same time, he cups my sex, then pulls me tighter against him.

He's trapped me there, holding me firmly against him by the pressure on both my mouth and my sex. I'm utterly at his whim. He could spread the panels of my skirt. He could lift it, completely exposing me. He could rip the lace of the bodice, releasing my aching nipples to the cool breeze that is blowing through these trees.

He could do all that, and for one moment of sanity, I think it is good that he's preventing me from speaking, because right then I might actually beg him to do all those things. Because I want that and more.

Hell, I want everything, and I squirm, moving my hips in a silent demand.

I feel the press of his erection against my rear and know that he wants it as well. That he's close, too. But I know Jackson, and I'm certain he won't go all the way. Not here. Not in this secluded dark corner.

But god help me, I want him to.

I arch my back so that my ass presses more intently against his crotch, then writhe against his cock as his fingers slide in to fill me. I feel my body clench around him, and shift back and forth, riding him, wanting his cock. Wanting him to come with me.

"Christ, Syl, stop. You don't know what you're doing to me." His voice at my ear is rough. But I do know what I'm doing. Of course I know what I'm doing. And to prove it to him, I slide my own hand between my legs and gently tug his fingers free.

From his throaty groan, I know that he can tell what I'm doing, and my assumption is confirmed when he says, "Are you sure?"

I answer in action and not words. I move my other hand between us and part the panels of the skirt that cover my backside.

"*Fuck*," he says, and the next thing I hear is the *snick* of his zipper. "Touch yourself," he orders. Then he's using his one hand to hold my skirt aside and the other to position himself. "Bend forward," he whispers. "Just a little."

I do, and then I have to swallow a cry when I feel the tip of his cock at my entrance for just an instant before he thrusts hard inside me.

"Baby, you feel so damn good," he says as one hand cups my breast and the other moves around to tease my clit. "Reach back and hold my hips."

I do as he demands, and he uses the pressure of my hands to keep us steady as he moves rhythmically inside me even as he teases my clit, so that I'm lost in a haze of glorious sensations.

Deeper and deeper, harder and harder. I'm whimpering, not ever wanting this to end—this sensation of spiraling upward toward something, and all the more exciting because there's a danger to it. A naughtiness. A wild intimacy that I can share only with Jackson.

"I'm close, baby," he murmurs, as the low timbre of his voice pushes me higher still. And then he explodes, his body convulsing, the wildness taking me over the edge, too, so that I shatter under the force of the electric shock that consumes my body, breaking me apart and sending me floating off out into the night.

And Jackson's strong arms are the only thing that hold me together and tether me to earth.

Chapter 8

SUNDAY SHOULD BE a lazy day, but since Jackson and I both took Friday off, we're playing catch-up before most people have taken their first sip of coffee.

The plan is to get all of our various ducks in a row for Monday, then get back home just after lunch so we can spend the afternoon with the kids at the children's museum.

We both work in Stark Tower—me on the twenty-seventh floor where Stark Real Estate Development is located, and Jackson on twenty-six, the floor he's sublet for the Los Angeles office of his own operation, Steele Development.

But he's not here now. He dropped me off, then continued on to Pasadena where he's meeting Wyatt, who's shooting the marketing photos for a office building that Jackson designed and for which I'm the project manager. The marketing plan has been moved up by two weeks, and so we need the images ready to go by early next week so we can start pre-leasing the property. They're going to do the shoot, and then Jackson is meeting with the leasing agent we've retained to walk her through the property and go over the various specs.

As for me, since I pretty much ate and drank my way through the weekend, I go first to the fitness center on twenty. I don't love running, but I figure twenty minutes on the treadmill followed by another half hour on the weight machines will do me a world of good.

I'm a sweaty mess when I finish, but I'm feeling pretty good about myself as I make my way through the gym to the women's locker room for a quick shower. There's only one other person in the gym today: Noah Carter, a red-haired tech genius who's been spending a lot of time in the offices lately doing some consulting work for Stark Applied Technology. He has the rugged good looks of someone who grew up on a farm, and a kind of silent aloofness that has the single women in the office speculating about him over coffee.

I don't usually play those games, but with Noah, I can't help but think that someone hurt him deeply. And considering the complete lack of interest he's shown in his speculating coworkers, I assume that the someone was a woman.

Today, he nods politely as I pass him on my way to get cleaned up. And although I consider asking if he wants to walk down to the coffee cart just outside the building, by the time I come back out, showered and dressed, he's gone.

I shrug, then head to my floor, passing the new weekend receptionist on my way. I'm so lost in thought that I almost miss her calling my name.

"Did you need me?" I ask, stopping just past her desk and turning around.

"I said that a messenger brought your purse. Apparently you left it at the Segel party last night." She sighs. "Was it amazing?"

"Yeah," I say with a distracted frown. "It was great. But I didn't leave my purse." I'm sure of it, because I popped over to Stella's bungalow this morning to see the kids, and I gave her a fifty so she could get a few extra things from the grocery store.

"Oh, you did," says the girl, whose name I don't recall. She lifts a beaded clutch from behind the desk and sets it on the desktop. I reach for it with a frown. "See? Your driver's license is even clipped to the outside."

Sure enough, someone has secured my driver's license to the purse with a giant black binder clip.

And that's especially odd because although that's not my purse, it is definitely my license. And how did my license get out of the little window in my wallet? I can barely get it out myself when I need to, it sticks so much to the clear plastic.

Definitely weird.

"Thanks," I say, my tone distracted as I take the purse and the clip and the license to my office. I open the clutch as I walk, thinking that maybe I fumbled my license after one too many drinks, and it fell near this clutch. The story doesn't ring true, however, not in small part because I didn't get drunk last night.

And even if I had dropped the license, why would someone deliver it to the office, instead of to the home address printed on it?

I'm completely baffled until I actually open the purse. That's when I see the envelope. In the envelope are photographs.

And the photographs are of me.

IT WAS A JOY to work with competent people, Jackson thought, as he watched Wyatt set up for a series of shots from a completely new angle.

Usually, Jackson had to be both architect and art director, but Wyatt knew his stuff, and Jackson had learned on the last couple of projects they'd worked on together to simply give Wyatt a general sense of what Jackson wanted, and then let the photographer run with it.

Each time, Wyatt came up with images even better than what Jackson had imagined.

Which was why Jackson was now simply letting the man work while he scrolled through his phone, answering key emails and shooting others to his assistant, Lauren, to handle.

He'd just lifted the phone to dictate a text when the sharp trill of his ringtone startled him. He glanced at the screen, saw it was Sylvia, and smiled as he answered it.

"I miss you already," he said without preamble. "I think we'll be done by lunch. Can you get away for a meal with your husband?"

"*Jackson.*"

The tightness in her voice erased his smile. He stiffened, turning his back automatically to Wyatt for privacy. "What?" he demanded. "Sylvia, what's wrong?"

"They're back. Oh, god, Jackson. I told you I was afraid they'd come back, and now they have."

For a moment, he had absolutely no idea what she was talking about. Then reality hit him full force across the head, making him stumble backward. "The photos?"

"Dozens of them. Not the clean ones he used for advertisements. The ones he took between. When we were alone. When he—" Her voice broke, and Jackson realized his hand was so tight around his phone that he was on the verge of cracking the case. "When he touched me," she finished in a trembling voice.

"What? How?"

"They're vile, Jackson. Horrible and—" He heard her draw a breath and imagined her sitting up straighter. "No. Never mind."

"Dammit, Syl. How did you get them? Who sent them?"

"It's okay. I'm okay. I'll tell you later."

"I'll be right there. Half an hour. Maybe less." Traffic was light. Surely he could get from this part of Pasadena to downtown in thirty minutes.

"No, please. Don't." She sounded calmer. Stronger. "I'm fine. Really. I just needed to hear your voice."

"Bullshit. I'm on my way."

"Dammit, Jackson, listen to me. There's nothing you can do. They're just photos. I have no idea who sent them or why. They're here, and you coming won't change that. But today's the only day that Terry can meet with you about the marketing campaign. Come to me, and the entire project gets thrown off schedule. And for what?"

He wanted to say that the *for what* was her. Being with her. Holding her. Helping her.

But he also knew she was right. More than that, he could hear the growing strength in her voice as she shifted to work mode. Focusing on her job, her priorities, and shoving to the back the noise of those horrible images of her childhood.

Work was a balm—hell, he knew that better than anyone. Hadn't he thrown himself into his work when Syl had walked away from him, in those years before he'd fought to get her back?

And when he *had* gotten her back, hadn't he made it his utmost priority to help her fight the demons that had ripped her away from him in the first place?

Now she was once again fighting the battle, and from what he could hear in her voice, she was winning. And though he wanted more than anything to wrap his arms around her and hold her close, he also knew that if he really wanted to help her, he had to let her make the choice of what to do next.

"Jackson?"

"I'm here, baby."

"Just meet me at home after your meeting, okay? There's nothing you can do this second. And there's no reason for you to rush. What would be the point?" she added. "After all, you're already here with me. You're always with me."

He closed his eyes and breathed deep. "I love you."

"I know. That's kind of my point."

He laughed. How the hell could she be making him laugh now?

He forced his voice to stay even, then promised he'd see her at home before ending the call. Then he bent over, hands to his knees, as he drew in breath after breath and fought the urge to beat the living shit out of someone.

But who? Who the hell had done this? And why?

"Jackson?"

Wyatt's voice surprised Jackson, and had him spinning around, his body tense, ready to lash out or repel a blow.

Wyatt stepped back, hands up in defense. "Whoa, man. What's going on?"

Immediately, Jackson sagged, the fight leaving him, replaced by a bone deep frustration and an equally potent worry. "Sorry. I'm just a little on edge."

Wyatt's eyes dipped to the phone in Jackson's hand. "Everything okay?"

"That was Syl. Apparently Robert Cabot Reed is reaching out from his fucking grave," Jackson added bitterly.

"Come again?"

But Jackson just waved the question away. He liked Wyatt, but how the hell could he explain without mentioning the pictures? The only thing the public knew about Reed's murder was that—supposedly—Douglas killed Reed to stop the movie about Jackson, the Fletcher House, and Ronnie's birthmother. Sylvia's hell wasn't on the public's radar, and Jackson intended to keep it that way.

"Never mind," he said. "It's all okay."

Wyatt nodded slowly. "I used to admire the guy's work as a photographer. Even have some of the ad shots he took in my collection. But I lost all respect for the bastard not long ago."

"Because of his threats to make the movie?"

"That was part of it. There were other reasons. Things I learned about the man."

Jackson nodded slowly, his mouth tight. "I don't know what you heard. But if it was vile, then my guess is your information is one-hundred percent accurate."

Wyatt's brow furrowed. "Are you sure you're okay?"

"I'm fine. Really."

Wyatt didn't look convinced. "I'm all done here," he said. "Why don't you go see your wife?"

"I would if she'd let me. I'm supposed to meet Terry here. Sylvia scheduled the meeting, and now she's pulling rank, telling me she's going to head home, but I have to stay put."

Wyatt chuckled. "Well, she is the project manager."

"Yes, she is," Jackson said, the pride in his voice genuine.

"I'll leave you to that, then." He glanced at his watch and frowned. "We got some great shots. And I know we're on a tight schedule, so I'll get them to you by tomorrow."

"Perfect." Jackson peered more closely at Wyatt's face. "You look a little pale. Feeling okay?"

"Just a bit of a time crunch," Wyatt said. "But trust me. Compared to the problems you're facing, I'm absolutely fine."

Chapter 9

I'M PACING SO much that it's a good thing we have tile in the downstairs rooms, because if there was carpet I'd have worn a hole in it.

The purse with the photos is on the kitchen table, and I'm going back and forth between the kitchen and the great room, hoping the motion will calm my nerves. Trying to convince myself not to call Jackson.

I'd told him I could handle this, and I'd meant it. But now I'm home. I'm alone. And it's all just weighing down on me.

I don't want to call him back, because I know he'll drop everything and come to me. But I have to talk, and so I dial Cass, then curse when I get her voice mail. "Something happened. I'm okay. Or I'm not. I don't know. Anyway, just call when you can."

I end the call, and just seconds later, the doorbell chimes. For a second, I actually think it's Cass, but that idiotic thought is immediately replaced with a more worrisome one—that my visitor is the person who left the photos.

I calm almost immediately, though. Only friends and

family on our permanent list can enter the neighborhood without being announced. Even messengers have to be cleared through. I don't know who it is. But I can't imagine it's my tormenter. And though I'm really not in the mood for company, since I'd sent Stella to the park with the kids, I head to the front hall to answer the door.

It's Wyatt, and he's standing on the front step looking so agitated that my concern for him almost overshadows my own fears.

"What's wrong?" I ask, then immediately backtrack to, "Come in, come in. Is something wrong? Is it Jackson?"

"No," he says, looking stiff and awkward as he comes inside. "I mean, he's upset. After your call …"

He trails off, and I look sharply at him. "What did he say?"

"Just that Reed's reaching out from the grave. I'm sure he figures I'll assume it's about the movie. But Syl," he continues, his voice thin, "I don't think it's about the movie. I think it's about those pictures of you."

I THINK IT'S about those pictures of you.

My body goes clammy and I see more than hear his words. They're like red neon flashing on the ceiling. Like the walls in *The Shining* oozing blood. Like some horrible blunt weapon meant to destroy me.

Because there are only a very few people who I'm certain know about those pictures of me. My dad. Jackson. Me. And, of course, whoever left me that purse.

Wyatt?

Oh, dear god, no. It can't be Wyatt.

I take a step backwards, my head shaking in denial. For

a moment, his expression is confused. Then his eyes widen and he steps toward me, his hand held out as I squeal and he says, "No! Oh, Syl, no, no! It's not me."

I freeze, uncertain, scared, totally freaked out.

He stops dead in front of me, his hands raised. "I swear. Christ, you know me. I would never—" He draws a harsh breath, clenches his hands into fists, and looks at me. "But the thing is, I think I know who is behind it."

"Who?" My voice is wary, but the truth is that I believe him. This is the man who's given me and Nikki photography lessons. Who's been a friend for years. Who I really can't imagine would ever hurt me like that.

"Mila. Mila Sanchez."

I stare at him. "What?" I finally say. "Are you kidding me? Why would you even—"

"She found the pictures at my studio." He holds up a hand to stop me before I can ask what the fucking hell those pictures were doing at his studio. "I bought fifty boxes of Reed's photographs at auction after his death. Blind boxes. Like a grab bag. I'd hadn't gone through them, but about a month ago, I decided I needed to sort them, keep what I wanted and toss the rest."

"What you wanted?"

"I'm a collector as well as a photographer," he explains. "Reed was a shit, but he did some amazing work, and I especially love the shots he took for ads. So I figured it was worth the investment. There weren't many bidders, actually, and so I ended up getting fifty boxes for under two grand."

I just nod, letting him continue.

"Anyway, I met Mila a while back when she working at

Damien's desk and was ordering a print of one of my originals that hangs just outside his office. We kept in touch, went out a few times, but nothing serious. It'd been months since I'd seen her, actually, but I've been working on a project lately, and I've been shooting a lot of models."

He shrugs, then shoves his hands in his pockets. "To be honest, she's not on my favorite person list—especially not after the way she talked shit about you after you fired her. Kept saying she wanted to find a way to get you back. Vindictive, but I figured it was just talk. And since she has a particular look—a dark feline quality—I called and asked her to do a few test shots at my studio one Saturday a few weeks ago. We ended up talking about the boxes. She offered to help me catalog them."

"Go on," I say, beginning to see where this is going.

"Your photos were in one of the boxes. I saw them," he adds, not quite meeting my eyes. "And so did she."

"Oh." I lick my lips.

"I'm so sorry, Syl. For what that bastard did, and for the fact that I've invaded your privacy."

I try to speak, but my throat is too thick.

"I should have told you sooner, but I honestly didn't know what to say. And I had no idea that she'd taken the photos. I only know now because I put two and two together after you called Jackson."

"Oh, god," I mutter. I'm pacing. Agitated. "This is a nightmare."

"I know," his voice is calm, like he's talking to a caged animal. "Reed was horrible. When I saw those photos, I knew they had power. I wanted to—"

"*Wanted to what, you goddamn sonofabitch?*"

Jackson's harsh voice startles both of us and we turn toward the front hall to find Jackson barreling toward Wyatt. I suck in a breath, certain my husband is about to plow his fist into Wyatt's face.

"Jackson, no!" I hear the words in the air, and I'm honestly not sure if they're mine or Wyatt's, or the mingled sound of both.

Jackson has Wyatt by the collar, and I see Wyatt's fist tighten in defense. Then Jackson shoves him back before turning sharply, grabbing a small glass vase, and slamming it into the ground, touchdown style.

The glass shatters, and I scream. "Stop it! Stop it! It's not Wyatt. Dammit, Jackson, Wyatt didn't send the pictures."

The men are staring at each other and my heart is pounding, not only because of what just happened, but because of what might still be yet to come. Jackson's temper is a wild thing, and I've already come close to losing him once.

Before we were together, he punched the screenwriter assigned to the movie about the Fletcher house. And once he knew what Reed did to me, he beat the crap out of him. Not only was Jackson arrested for assault, but that breach of temper was one of the reasons he'd been the prime suspect in Reed's later murder. A crime he probably would have gone to jail for had my father not confessed.

Another fight—another arrest—and he might end up serving jail time for assault. And goddammit, I can't lose this man.

"Calm down!" I demand, my voice not yet calm. "It wasn't him! Wyatt came here to help. He knows who sent the photos."

"Who?" Jackson growls, still looking like he wants to beat the shit out of someone. But at least he's holding himself in check.

I draw a breath as I meet Wyatt's eyes. "Mila Sanchez."

"*Bitch.*" He steps to the left, moving back toward the door, and I move quickly to take his arm.

"No," I say, certain that he was about to head right back out to go find Mila.

"The hell you say. We need to go have a little talk with Mila about her manners."

"Dammit, Jackson, no. Not yet. I want a plan. And, goddammit, I want you calm." Because there is no way we're walking into her apartment with Jackson as hyped up as he is. I want *Mila* to be the one getting into trouble. Not Jackson.

He says nothing, but the muscle twitch in his cheek and the set of his jaw is answer enough. The man is seriously *not* happy.

"Promise me," I say.

"How long?" I can hear the control he's working to keep in his voice.

"Tomorrow," I say. "I just want to think. I don't want to go in hot. She'll expect that."

He nods slowly, already calming. "She will. You're right." He draws another breath, then looks at Wyatt. "Sorry."

"I get it," Wyatt says. "And since you pulled your punch, we're all good."

Jackson chuckles. "So what the fuck? How does she have these pictures? How are you involved?" he asks Wyatt. "And what the hell is her endgame?"

Wyatt explains what he'd told me. As for the endgame, though, he looks at me. I shrug. "She doesn't like me. Maybe she just wants to have one over on me."

"No," Jackson says with certainty. "We're still waiting for the other shoe to drop."

He's probably right, I think, as Wyatt says that he's going to leave us alone. "I should have come sooner," he adds. "And I'm so, so sorry."

"Wyatt—" Jackson begins, his voice gritty with apology.

"It's okay, man. I get it. Really." He turns and heads for the front door, not waiting for us to reply.

Jackson stalks toward me, circumventing the glass on the floor, and I see the fire in his face. Anger. Need. Concern.

"Whoever did this. Whoever sent you those goddamn photos, I'll—"

"Jackson, we—"

But I don't finish the sentence. He pulls me to him, silencing me with a hard, consuming kiss. My pulse kicks up. My skin burns. I want his touch. Want *him*. Christ, how much I want him. But it's heat. It's desire.

It's not from fear.

And it's not because I'm lost, knocked under by the threats against me.

The realization startles me, and I gasp, pushing away so that I can look in his eyes.

"I'm okay," I say, the words full of amazement.

I see the acknowledgement on his face along with the desire. And, yes, an undercurrent of wild, untamed pain.

"I'm not." His words are growl. A confession. A demand.

And that's when full understanding hits me. I *want* this—his touch, his heat—but Jackson *needs* it. He told me once that he channeled anger into fighting, and the scar across his eyebrow that I find so damn sexy is only one remnant of that trait.

So I understand what he's saying now. He needs to cool the fear and the anger. He needs to lash out. To go wild.

I want him to go wild with me. More than that, I know he wants it too. My submission. My surrender.

"Jackson." His name is soft. Barely a breath. But he hears the invitation, and his groan of power and passion cuts through me, firing all my senses.

He spins me around, then pulls my shirt off. Next, he slides my gray jersey skirt down my hips. It's a favorite of mine, casual and comfortable, and now it pools around my ankles. "Kick it off," he orders. "Kneel on it. Leave the shoes on. Hands on your thighs."

I do as he asks, going down on my knees on my skirt in front of him. "Eyes closed," he says. Again I comply, and when he speaks again, to say simply, "Good girl," his voice sounds farther away.

He must not have gone far, though, because within moments, he's back, and he puts something soft over my eyes. For a moment, I'm confused, then realize it must be one of the decorative scarves I keep in the drawer of the contemporary-style chest that is the focal point of the foyer.

He ties it firmly, then tells me to lift my hands. I do, and he positions my fingers on his fly. I know what he wants, of course. But it's not just my mouth on his cock. He wants to demand it. He wants me to obey. And so I wait, more than willing to play this game. Excited by it, in fact, as I'm sure he can tell from the way my nipples are tight against the thin lace of my bra.

My breathing is ragged, and I'm desperately wet. I want this as much as he does. I want to give myself to him. To submit to him. Not because I need it in order to fight off childhood demons, but because I want the pleasure it gives both of us. The satisfaction that my submission gives him, and the glorious sensation of being free that it gives me. The undiluted pleasure of a trust so pure I can go to the limit, balance on the precipice, and know that I will always be safe because Jackson will never push me too far.

"Go on, baby," he says, his voice rough. "You know what I want."

I do, and I carefully unbutton his slacks and then ease down the zipper of his fly. He's rock hard, and I draw his cock out, stroking the length of him before easing forward and teasing the tip with my tongue as my hand curves around his shaft, stroking in slow, steady motions.

He groans, the sound deepening when I draw his cock into my mouth. And though I've started out slowly, teasing him and playing with him, it's soon clear that he has no intention of letting me remain in control. His fingers cup my head, and he holds me steady, then thrusts into me, fucking my mouth. Giving me no respite. Silently demanding that I take it—take *him.*

And oh, dear lord, I love it.

I can feel the thrusts through every inch of my body. A wild burning that seems to start in my blood and seep out to my skin. That fires me up and makes me burn. I want his hands on me. I want his cock inside me. I want to take him all the way, to feel him explode in my mouth, and then

I want to use my hands and tongue and teeth to bring him back. To make him hard. And ride him this time until our bodies are fused together and whatever explosion comes take us both over the edge and spinning off into space, trapped together in each other's arms.

He's close—so very, very close. And I think that I'm going to have my wish.

But then he pulls my head back away from his body, leaving me gasping and unsure. The scarf is still around my eyes and though I hear movement, I don't know what he's doing. I'm completely aroused, the thong panties I still wear totally soaked.

"I want to be inside you," he whispers, stoking the flames inside me once more.

And the next thing I know, I'm in his arms, and he's carrying me. Then he's lowering me to his lap, and I'm straddling him. He's still dressed, and I fist my hands in his shirt even as his mouth finds mine. The kiss is hard and hot and deep, and I squirm in his lap, rubbing myself against his erection until I don't think I can stand it anymore.

Apparently he can't either, because he reaches between our bodies, tugs the thong aside with one hand, and growls, "Now, dammit, Syl. I have to be inside you now."

I need no more encouragement, and I ease down, taking him in, biting my lower lip in defense against the wonderfully sweet sensation of this man filling me. And then, as if he can't take it anymore, he grabs my hips and pushes me down, impaling me on his erection. I cry out in surprise, then gasp and arch back wanting to feel all of him. Hell, wanting to simply *feel*.

His fingers tease my clit as I rise and fall, but it's when

his hand snakes behind and his fingertip teases my anus that I really lose my mind.

"Take off the blindfold," he demands, and when I do, I see the heat in his eyes and know that it matches mine. "Touch yourself with me," he says, urging my finger down to curl around his as he strokes my clit, my pussy so warm and slick.

I moan and start to close my eyes. "No," he orders. "Watch me." And I do. My eyes on his as he teases me—as *we* tease me. My hips rising and falling. My body on fire from all of the assaults on my senses. And then, when he claims my mouth and takes me hard—when his finger slips hard into my ass even as his fingertip brushes my clit with a featherlight touch—the cacophony of sensation is too much for me, and I break apart, my body throbbing as my cunt clenches hard around him, milking him, desperate to take him over the edge, too.

And when he arches back and groans, I know I've succeeded. "Me," I demand. "Look at me." He does. And I hold his gaze as the two of us lose ourselves to passion in each other's arms.

Later, when reason has returned and I can breathe again, I curl next to him, safe and satisfied in the circle of his arms. "I love you," he whispers, and I draw in the words like oxygen, understanding the unspoken message, too—that he will always protect me.

"I thought it was over," I whisper. "After my dad, I mean. I thought all the bullshit about those pictures—about Reed—I thought it was done." I shift in his arms to face him. "But it's never really done, is it?"

Jackson kisses my forehead gently. "I don't know, baby. I just don't know."

Chapter 10

"THAT FUCKING BITCH!" Cass says, the moment I slide into her favorite booth at the Blacklist Bar.

I grimace, then take a long swallow of my martini. Cass has already ordered for us—and is on her second drink, since my drive is longer than her walk. She'd finally called me back. And since Jackson understands the extent of our BFF bond, he'd kissed me hard and told me to go meet her. Since he'd seemed calmer—especially after an hour of playing with the kids—I'd agreed.

Blacklist Bar is a Venice Beach icon. Since it's located just a few doors down from Totally Tattoo, it's also Cass's favorite after-work hang-out. According to the back of the cocktail menu, the bar has been around since the nineteen-thirties, but didn't acquire its current name until the sixties when the name was changed as an homage to the blacklisted movie stars who became regulars during the age of McCarthyism.

I have absolutely no idea if the story is even a little bit true, but I do know that the bartenders are friendly, the happy hour is awesome, and the kitchen makes the best cheese fries on the planet.

Today, however, I'm having a hard time enjoying either the alcohol or the carbs, and I poke my last olive with the plastic toothpick as Cass tells me over and over again that she just can't believe what happened.

"That bitch," she says for the umpteenth time, the anger in her eyes as red and fierce as today's hair. "That psycho *bitch*."

"Not arguing," I say.

"That explains the constipated look on her face when I saw her the other day. I just figured it was because you'd fired her delusional, troublemaking ass."

"I'm thinking now that might have been a mistake." I stab the olive, then pop it into my mouth. "What's that saying about keeping your enemies close?"

"Yeah, but then you'd have to hang out with her. And can I just say—Mila? Not such great company."

Despite myself, I grin.

"So what are you going to do?"

I shake my head. "Honestly, I don't know. I mean, all she's done so far is send me a purse full of pictures."

"She's up to something," Cass says darkly.

"Not exactly news," I say. "I'm just waiting for the other shoe to drop."

"How's Jackson?"

"Holding his temper in check."

"That's something," she says, and we clink glasses in girlfriend solidarity.

When we finish our drinks, she suggests we walk back to her place. "We can chill on the back porch. And Siobhan gets off work soon. I know she'd love to see you."

I want to get home to Jackson and the kids, but I haven't seen Siobhan in ages, so I agree. We settle the bill, then head out, talking about nothing in particular as we hit the street. I'm grateful, because for the first time all day, the photos aren't at the forefront of my mind.

"I feel like I'm breaking a marriage code," I joke. "Me, off drinking. And Jackson stuck at home with the kids."

Cass rolls her eyes. "Don't even pretend like you don't want to be right there with him. I know I'm sloppy seconds. I can deal. I'm not developing a complex. I'm not—"

I expect something biting and funny. Instead, she goes silent, squeezing my hand hard.

"Cass—" Her name is a protest, and I start to yank my hand free. Then I see her face—and the direction she's looking.

My car. My little Nissan I've had forever, that never did anything to anybody, is covered in black splotches of paint. And all four tires are brutally slashed.

Bile rushes up my throat and I rip my hand free before being violently ill in the street.

"Syl!" Cass holds me, then yells a vulgarity at a pedestrian who's decided to stop and stare. "Come on," she says, starting to hurry me away.

I fight back, digging in my heels.

"Dammit, Syl. Come to the shop." She gestures toward Totally Tattoo. "You don't need to stay out here and torture yourself."

"Note," I say. "Get the note."

At first she just looks confused. Then her face clears as she notices what I'd seen early on. A manila envelope under the windshield with big block letters on the outside: *Sylvia.*

With a sound that is almost a snarl, Cass snatches the note, then clutches it so tightly her knuckles are white. She takes my elbow and we hurry to the shop. It's closed now, but she takes us in through the back, and I plunk myself down on the ratty sofa that's been in the business office since her dad owned the place.

"I don't want to read it," I say.

"I think you have to." Her voice is full of distaste.

I nod. "I know. But will you—I mean, can you read it out loud?"

She makes a face, but nods, then uses a letter opener to slowly rip the edge of the envelope open. After that, she turns it upside down and shakes it, sending a page of notebook paper ripped from a spiral drifting to the ground.

She picks it up with a tissue, and I roll my eyes. "We don't need to worry about fingerprints," I point out. "We know who did it."

"You can never be too careful," she retorts.

I shrug. At this point, I don't even want to know what the note says, much less think about why we'd want to preserve fingerprints. But when she waits just a little too long to start reading, I snap, "Oh, go on, already," then close my eyes as this newest blow comes.

"Tuesday," Cass says in a tight, clear voice. "Four p.m. Five-hundred thousand to the account below. Or by Wednesday, you'll be the newest internet sensation." She exhales loudly as she looks up at me. "And there are wiring instructions on the bottom," she adds, then lashes out with, "*Bitch.*"

I keep my eyes closed as I count to ten. I feel alternatively hot and cold, and I have to keep pushing back the overwhelming sensation to just take off running, not stopping until I'm all the way back to the Palisades and safe in Jackson's arms.

Jackson. Oh, god, Jackson.

I want him so desperately it's a physical need, but I force it back. *I can handle this. I can be strong.*

I swallow, then nod to myself. I've got this.

I meet Cass's eyes, my hand extended. "Let me see." She passes it to me, along with a fresh tissue. I ignore it and tug the paper free with my fingertips.

I skim it, my stomach churning. The idea of paying half a million in blackmail makes me sick. But the idea of having those photos out in the wild cuts even deeper. Forget the simple fact that I don't want my privacy invaded, I also don't want to slide backward, falling down into a dark, emotional quagmire again. Yes, I have Jackson now, and he will always catch me when I fall, but I don't want to be in the position in the first place. And it pisses me off to realize that I'm still so damned fragile.

Cass takes my hand. "It's going to be okay."

"Is it?" A sudden shudder cuts through me. "The thought that those pictures might get out—that she'll profit if they don't—"

I realize that my hand is going numb, and when I look down, I see that Cass is clutching my wrist so tight that her knuckles are white. "You have to go to the police," she says. "This is malicious. She vandalized your car. Christ, she used a knife. Next time she might use it on you."

I shake my head. "No. No police."

"Syl! You have to—"

"*No.*" My voice is more shrill than I'd intended, and I

draw a breath trying to calm down. "Don't you get it? Once the police are involved, there are eyes all over it. It's not a question of *if* the photos will leak, but *when.*" My words are harsh, but for the first time, I realize that it's anger, not fear. I'm pissed. Royally and totally pissed that this woman has so much power over me because I was a victim. And now here I am, a victim once again.

"It's fucked," I say calmly. "But I'm not going to the police." I draw a breath. "I know what I have to do."

Her brows knit into a V over her nose. "Are you going to kill her?" she deadpans, and despite myself, I burst out laughing.

"That's why I love you," I say. "But no."

She makes a face. "Too bad. Of course, Jackson might." She's teasing, but there's a hint of worry beneath it, and I nod in understanding. And fear.

After all, he'd almost pounded Wyatt on nothing more than a suspicion. And while I might enjoy watching Mila get the shit kicked out of her, losing his temper might mean destroying our family. Because Jackson's already been arrested for assault once, and I doubt they'll accept a plea the second time around.

Frankly, I don't want my kids only knowing their daddy from behind a glass visitor's window.

Cass is studying my face. "You don't really think he'd—"

"No," I say quickly, though I wish I were more certain. "He wouldn't hurt a woman. Not even a bitch like Mila." But what if she baits him? His temper is famous. What if she goads him because she wants him to hit her? Because she wants to fuck with us?

The possibility makes me twitchy.

"So what are you going to do?" Cass asks.

I suck in a breath. "I'm going to go talk to her. I'm going to make her understand that her perfect little world will come to a screeching halt if she releases those photos. Because I'm married to a powerful man who's the brother of an even more powerful man. And if those pictures see the light of day, I will happily, enthusiastically, and with complete and total joy, sic them both on her and tell them to do their worst."

I grimace. "Or I might just chicken out and pay." Because threats aren't a sure thing, and she might decide to brave their wrath and release the pictures anyway.

Cass nods slowly, obviously considering my words. "Well, I guess you'll decide when you decide. You'll probably have an idea of how well the threat plan will work when you're in a room with her, up close and personal with the crazy bitch."

"That's what I figure."

"But you know you can't go alone."

I tilt my head. "I appreciate the offer, but you're not going with me."

"Not me, though I'll come in a heartbeat if you need me there. I'm talking about Jackson. Threaten her with your husband and brother-in-law's power, and he needs to be there. Pay her, and you need to tell him. Because I think one of the rules of marriage goes something like 'Thou shalt not spend half-a-million dollars without telling thouest spouse.'"

"Thouest?"

She rolls her eyes, and I realize I'm actually grinning. A

little.

But at least I have a plan, and I can't deny that feels good.

"Of course I'm taking him," I say.

But then Cass goes and crushes my moment of levity. "If he loses his temper, it's not going to be good. He dodged a bullet once. Remind him that he may not be able to dodge it again."

And that, I think, is very good advice.

Hopefully, Jackson will heed it.

Chapter 11

"THIS IS IT," Jackson says, as he slides his Porsche into a slot in front of Mila's apartment in Silver Lake. It's dark now, and the two nearest streetlights are burned out. But even so, I can make out his face when he turns to look at me. And though his expression is both protective and supportive, I can see the fury boiling beneath the surface.

I'd called him from Totally Tattoo and while he'd held it together—barely—when he'd read the note and seen the car, I almost wish he'd lost it on the street. Because I know it's all building up inside him. And somehow, someway, it's all going to explode.

"Ready?" he asks, and my stomach twists with nerves.

I want to tell him that he's the one who needs to be ready. That he has to keep it together. But he already knows that, and I trust him.

Dear god, I hope I'm not wrong to trust him…

"Syl?"

"Yes," I say stoutly. "I'm ready."

He opens the door, and the overhead light comes on so that I can see him clearly when he pauses to look back at me. "It's going to be fine," he says, and I nod in agreement.

But whether he's reassuring me about the photos or his temper, I really don't know.

I reach for my door handle, then hesitate. "When we see her, let me do the talking, okay?"

"Afraid I'll lose my temper?" he asks with a grin, because of course he knows that's worrying me even though I haven't said a word since we left Venice Beach.

"It's my life she's stomping all over," I say, dodging the question. "My pain she's treating so cavalierly. And that means this is something I have to do."

"I know, baby," he says, then squeezes my hand. "I won't say a word. But I'm coming in with you." He brushes his fingertips over my jaw. "And not just because you need me there, but because I need to be there, too."

"I do need you," I say, feeling some of the tension drain out of me. "You're what makes me strong."

His smile is both gentle and encouraging. "No," he says. "You've always been strong. I'm just the man who helped you realize it."

MILA'S APARTMENT IS on the first floor near the back, and we walk past the empty laundry room and a small pool before we reach it.

We stand in the circle of anorexic light cast by her porch light, and Jackson keeps a supportive hand on my back as I rap hard on the door. For a moment, there is simply silence, and I fear that she's not home. But then I hear footsteps, the jangle of someone pulling aside a chain, and then the click of a deadbolt unlocking.

A second later, the door opens, revealing Mila standing there in a skin-tight tank top and ass-revealing cut-offs, her expression hard and calculating. And I don't care what Wyatt says; it's not a feline face at all. That would be an insult to cats.

"Oh," she says, her eyes hard on me. "It's you. Come to fire me again?"

"I would if I could, believe me. But no. I'm here to talk. Can we come in?"

She crosses her arms over her chest, sighs, then steps aside. "Whatever."

I glance at Jackson, who takes my hand and gives it a little squeeze for support. Then we step into her lair.

"So, why are you here? Come to apologize?"

I cock my head to the side and force my temper down. She's either completely innocent or she's a pathological, practiced liar. My money's on the second.

"Well?" she demands when I don't respond immediately.

"No apology," I say. "Just a warning."

"Yeah? About what?"

"About not trying to cut corners, Mila. Blackmail's a nasty way to make a living. It really never works out."

Her lips thin so much they almost disappear. "I don't know what you're talking about," she says icily.

"I'm pretty sure you do," I say. "But since I'm not one-hundred percent sure about your intelligence, I'll run it down for you anyway."

She looks like she's going to snarl, but I just keep talking.

"You were at Wyatt's house. You found the photos. You decided you'd get revenge on me for firing you and score a little cash at the same time. Well, guess what, Mila, it won't work. You're not getting paid. And if you release those photos, your ass is going to end up behind bars. You know who I'm married to," I say, glancing at Jackson. "You know who my brother-in-law is. And you know what they can do."

"Don't you threaten me," she snaps, but while she sounds angry, her eyes look scared. "Someone's blackmailing you because of some photos?"

"Yeah," I snap. "And that someone is you."

"Sorry, chica, but you're all kinds of fucked in the head."

I squeeze Jackson's hand. Because right now, I'm tempted to lash out and smack her across the face myself.

Mila cocks her head. "And as for finding some bullshit pictures at Wyatt's studio, in case you weren't clued in, that boy has a revolving door policy. You visiting every one of those girls personally?"

"No. Just the ones I fired. Just the ones who want revenge."

"Bitch. I didn't do anything to you. And you know what else? I don't like you. Or your asshole of a bodyguard either," she adds, with a nod toward Jackson. "But just because I don't like you doesn't mean I'm out to get you. You can't prove shit. And if you keep on harassing me, then whoever really is blackmailing you is going to be pissed off and release the damn photos when they don't get their money."

The problem of course is that she's right. Not that she's not the blackmailer, but about how it could all play out.

I can pay, and hope she keeps her word.

I can walk away with the threat hanging over Mila, and hope that she believes that there's a jail cell in her future.

But if she thinks she can hide behind the other women in Wyatt's life—or if she's not the blackmailer at all—the pictures might still be released.

All of that runs through my head.

And then the most remarkable thing happens. I realize that I don't care.

Well, I *care*. But not enough to pay off some bitch who's blackmailing me.

Not enough to turn my life and my emotions inside out.

Because the truth is, I'm okay. It's amazing. It's unexpected. But it's absolutely true, and it's been nagging at me since my father was released. The simple, inescapable fact that I didn't do anything wrong.

I've always known it. But now I feel it.

My father was in the wrong.

Reed sure as hell was.

But I was completely innocent.

Do I want those pictures out there? No, I don't. But if they are released, all they show is a girl who'd been taken advantage of. Whatever guilt I thought the world would see doesn't exist.

I don't want them released because I don't want the attention. Because they're private. Not because of guilt or of shame. I have nothing to be ashamed of, after all. Of all the people who brought those photos to light, I'm the only one who's guilt free.

"Are we done?" Mila's been staring at me warily as I gathered my thoughts. "You wanna get the fuck out of my apartment?"

"Actually, yes," I say. "I want to get as far away from you as I can." I conjure a broad, friendly smile. "But just so you're up to speed, I'm not paying you shit. And if the photos are released, then I'm okay with that. Because I can stand a little embarrassment if that's the price to see the shit storm that will rain down upon you when I tell the cops all that I know."

Her eyes go wide. "I told you! I didn't do it. I'm not the one who threatened you. And if you don't pay and those photos get released, don't you be blaming me."

"Shut up, Mila. We both know it's you, even if you don't want to say it. Trust me. Don't release the photos. It'll be much better for you if you don't. Oh, and Mila," I add sweetly as we pause at the door, "you might want to consider moving. You've read about Jackson's temper, right?"

She swallows, and I shrug. "It's just that you really do have a pretty face," I say. "It would be a shame to mess it up."

I'm laughing as we hurry back toward the street, but my mirth is cut short when Jackson takes my arm and tugs me into the empty laundry room, then slams and locks the door.

"What are you—"

But it's not a question I need to ask, and when he presses me up against the washing machine and closes his mouth over mine, I'm not at all surprised. He'd held it in—the wildness, the anger, the fear for me. Now he's letting it go.

Now, he needs me. And god knows, I need him.

"Yes," I murmur when he pulls away, his eyes full of a heat that rages like wildfire.

Without a word, he yanks up my skirt, then rips off my thong panties. He lifts me effortlessly so that my ass is balanced on the edge of the machine, and as he lowers his zipper and takes out his cock, I wrap my legs tight around his waist.

He's hard—and I'm so damn wet—and he enters me in one quick thrust, making me arch back and gasp with pleasure. He doesn't kiss me, but we lock eyes as he pounds into me. As I hold on tight to the machine to steady myself and take it, thrust after punishing thrust, deep and wild as he works through it, turning the explosion of rage into a flood of passion. Using me to help him turn it around. Claiming me. Needing me.

Just like I've always needed him.

Just like we've always needed each other.

We explode together, and I collapse forward into his arms, my breath coming in wild gasps. And that's when I realize that this wild encounter was just as much for me as for him. Because I'd been holding it in—my fear that he would do something to Mila. That somehow, he'd screw up and erase everything we'd built.

I should have known better, and I cling to him, just wanting to feel him against me.

"You thought I'd lose it in there," he says, and I nod, feeling miserable. "Oh, baby," he says gently, "don't you know that I would never—*never*—lose my temper like that? Not anymore. Not after I came so close to being locked up away from you."

"I love you," I say as relief floods through me.

"That's kind of my point," he says, mimicking the words I'd said to him just the other day.

He helps me off the washing machine, then adjusts my skirt. My panties are toast, so he picks them up off the floor and tosses them in the trash. Then he just stands there looking at me as I run my hands over my clothes, making sure I'm decent before we step outside.

"What?" I say, narrowing my eyes.

A slow grin lights his face, giving him a devilishly sexy appeal. "You were brilliant," he says sincerely. "But you're taking a hell of a risk. She might still release them. Or she might not be the one."

"She is," I say. "I'm certain. And she won't release them."

"I actually agree with you on both counts. And you only got one thing wrong in there."

I tilt my head in question.

"I might spend a few pleasant moments fantasizing about rearranging her nose on that perky little face, but I wouldn't ever hit her. She's really not worth it."

I shrug. "Mila doesn't know that. Do you have a problem with making her sweat a little?"

His laugh fills the small room. "Nope," he says. "No problem at all." He turns the bolt and pulls the door open. "Home?"

I shake my head. "Not just yet. There's one more place I need to go."

Chapter 12

MY MOTHER ISN'T home when we arrive at my parents' San Diego house, and I'm not at all surprised. I'm sure she left the moment my father said we were coming. I feel a slight twinge of pain, like a pinch in my side, but I ignore it. I've wasted enough energy thinking about my mom. I'm not going to waste any more.

My dad, on the other hand, has clearly been anticipating our arrival. There's a bottle of wine on the small table in the kitchen along with a pot of coffee and a package of Chips Ahoy cookies.

"I remembered you liked them as a kid," he says. "I bought a pack when I went to the grocery store yesterday. Nice thing, being able to walk into a grocery store and buy what you want." He turns to Jackson. "Don't ever take it for granted."

"I won't," says Jackson, who came so close to being behind bars himself. "I don't."

"Turns out I like the damn cookies so much I ate the whole package last night while I was watching NFL replays on ESPN. So when you said you were coming down, I made another trip. Wouldn't want you to do without."

He says the whole speech without looking at me. Except for the bit about going back to the store.

"Thanks, Daddy," I say, and I mean it. "I still love the damn things."

He takes a deep breath, then slowly releases it. "So what is it you need to talk to me about? I suppose it's important if you're coming all the way down here in afternoon traffic."

"It is," I say, and watch as he seems to flinch.

"Daddy?"

"If you're going to keep me away from my grandkids, I won't argue. But spit it out and let's get past it."

I think about how vibrant Ronnie had been playing with her grandfather, and about how young and alive my father's face had been.

"No," I say, catching Jackson's eye to see if he shares my confusion. "No, that's not why we're here at all."

"Why would you think that?" Jackson asks, but I've already arrived at the answer, and blurt it out before my father can say it.

"Mother," I say flatly. I feel a fresh anger rising in me, and I tamp it down. I'm not here about that woman or her fabrications. But I am here for something real. "No," I say again. "It's just … well, it's just that the photos may come out." I tell him about the blackmail threat and how we've refused to pay.

"I'm okay with it," I assure him. "But, Daddy, when I made that decision … well, if those photos get out, it's going to erase what you did. You killed him to keep them hidden. You'll have killed him for nothing." My voice breaks a little. "I'm sorry about that. But I have to let them go." Beneath the table, Jackson squeezes my hand, and I draw strength from his touch. "I'm ready to let them go. More than that, I think I need to."

My father takes a bite of his cookie. "And you drove all the way down here to tell me that? Because you think I'm going to be upset?"

I lick my lips. "Aren't you? You served time to keep those photos hidden."

He sighs. "Aw, sweetheart. I appreciate that, I do. But none of this is about me. It's about you. However you can get past this, then you do that thing. Whatever it takes for you to realize it wasn't your shame, but Reed's. And mine. And your mother's."

I feel tears prick my eyes and look down at the hand that's still tight in Jackson's.

"Take out a billboard," my dad continues. "Call me out on Oprah. Whatever you need so that you can hold your head up high."

I nod, moved by his words. But in the end, there's really only one thing that I need. I shift in my chair so that I can see Jackson better, and find him looking back with a fierce and perfect intensity. *Him*, I think.

"I have it, Daddy," I whisper. "Thanks."

And for the first time in a very long time, I add one more thing. "I love you," I say. And I really mean it.

I WAKE IN a sensual haze, drawn from a sweet, dreamless sleep by Jackson's mouth teasing my breast and his strong hands holding me at the waist. My eyes flutter open and I look down to see the top of his head as his teeth tease my nipple.

Most mornings I greet the day feeling soft and refreshed. Not so today.

Now, I'm aroused, wild and needy, and I writhe beneath him, my hands gripping the sheets as a sensual heat cuts through every inch of my body. Craving more. Wanting everything.

Wanting Jackson.

"Yes," I murmur, spreading my legs in what I hope he takes as an invitation. I'm not disappointed, and with one final tug on my breast, he trails his kisses lower and lower, tracing a slow, wonderfully tortuous path to my core.

His hands slide upward taking over where his mouth had once been, and as his tongue teases my clit, his palms cup my breasts. Lightly, he pinches my nipples as his mouth rouses me to a fever pitch, taking me so close to the edge but never quite over it.

I arch up, my body searching for more. For release. But it's always just out of reach. And only when I know that I can't stand the torment one more second do I resort to begging, my plea nothing more than his name, since that's all I can manage in the form of sound.

He understands, though. And in proof that he was truly tormenting me—as evidence that he knows my body as intimately as I do—he slides his hand down and uses his tongue and his fingers to expertly and efficiently send me shooting off into space, my body trembling with the power of the orgasm that has been building and building, so that all I can do is ride it out, waiting until I break to pieces and fall back to the bed and into Jackson's arms.

I'm breathing hard when he eases up beside me, grins, and then kisses me sweetly. "Good morning," he says, making me laugh.

"A very good morning," I agree.

It's been a week since I told Mila that we wouldn't pay, and so far the photos haven't surfaced. "They still might," I'd told Jackson last night, but he'd just shaken his head.

"I don't think so," he'd said. "And even if they do, we'll be fine, just like you said. Because you're the strongest woman I know."

I think about those words now, because it's Jackson who makes me strong, and I lean in for another kiss. This time, however, I'm foiled by a rhythmic pounding at the door to our bedroom followed by a high pitched little voice demanding, "Mommy! Daddy! Why is the door locked?"

Jackson winks at me, then slides out of bed. He grabs a pair of pajama bottoms from atop the bench at the foot of the bed, then pulls them on after throwing me my nightgown. I get dressed, too, and once we're both decent, he opens the door.

Ronnie marches in, frowning. "It was locked," she announces.

"Sometimes mommies and daddies lock doors," Jackson explains as I move out of the room and down the hall to check on Jeffery. I can still hear them talking as I make silly faces while changing his diaper, then carry him back to the bedroom.

"But if it's locked, then how can I get in?" Ronnie is asking.

"You raise a very good question," Jackson says, and I bite back laughter.

"Jeffery!" Ronnie is in the middle of the bed, and now she bounces and starts covering and uncovering her eyes.

"Peek-eye," she says, then laughs and laughs when Jeffery mimics her, babbling "Ra-Ra!" as he does, which is Jeffery-speak for Ronnie.

"Put him here," she demands, and I defer to the princess's wishes and put Jeffery on the bed in front of her, between me and Jackson. I figure we have at least twenty minutes until he loses interest in his sister and howls for breakfast.

"Tell us a story, Daddy! Please!"

Jackson grins, then puts his arm out for me. I snuggle close so that the four of us make a tightly knit circle, then sigh as I think about my life and how very lucky I am.

"Once upon a time," he begins, "there was a brilliant and magical princess named Veronica—"

"Yay!" she interrupts, clapping her hands. "Does it end with happily ever after?"

"Of course," he says, with a soft glance toward me. "There's always a happily ever after."

The End

Read on for *Steal My Heart,*
a bonus short story included with this novella.

And be sure not to miss *Anchor Me,*
the fourth book in The Stark Trilogy!

FROM *NEW YORK TIMES* AND #1 INTERNATIONAL BESTSELLING AUTHOR J. KENNER comes the highly anticipated fourth novel in the fast-paced series including *Release Me*, *Claim Me*, and *Complete Me*. This sexy, emotionally charged romance continues the story of Damien Stark, the powerful multimillionaire who's never had to take "no" for an answer, and his beloved wife Nikki Fairchild Stark, the Southern belle who only says "yes" on her own terms.

It's a new chapter in the life of Nikki and Damien Stark …

Though shadows still haunt us, and ghosts from our past continue to threaten our happiness, my life with Damien is nothing short of perfection. He is my heart and my soul. My past and my future. He is the man who holds me together, and his love fuels my days and enchants my nights.

But when tragedy and challenge from both inside and outside the sanctity of our marriage begins to chip away at our happiness, I am forced to realize that even a perfect life can begin to crack. And if Damien and I are going to win this new battle, it will take all of our strength and love …

Want even more Nikki & Damien?

Be sure not to miss Entice Me

A Stark Ever After Novella

STEAL MY HEART

A Steele Short Story

Dear Readers—

This short story came about because *Deepest Kiss*, a Stark Ever After novella, is told from Nikki Fairchild Stark's point of view. And while Nikki might be Sylvia's friend and sister-in-law, she wasn't actually present when Sylvia went into labor or delivered Baby Steele at the end of that novella.

And if Nikki wasn't there, that means that you weren't there either. So this short story was written to fill a gap, and was originally offered as a free download to fans. I wanted to give readers a chance to see what was going on in Sylvia and Jackson's minds and hearts in the days before the baby's arrival. That's an important event, and I didn't want you to be left out!

I hope you enjoy this very quick read, which chronologically precedes *Take My Dare* … and be sure to check the list of all my other Stark titles to make sure you haven't missed any stories!

XXOO

J. Kenner

Chapter One

"THIS WAS SO great, you guys," I say as I stand in the bungalow's open doorway and hug my sister-in-law, Nikki Stark. "My only regret is that I didn't get to see Cass fondle a paper penis." Apparently my party-planning friends had decided that Pin the Sperm on the Egg was more appropriate for a baby shower than Pin the Penis on the Hunk.

My best friend, Cass, raises her newly pierced brow, making the little diamond studded bar sparkle. "Paper's the only kind I would fondle," she retorts, reaching for her girlfriend Siobhan's hand. "Now if you want to play pin the nipple on the breast…"

"Not even," I say, cringing. I'm only a few weeks from my due date, and my breasts are so full and heavy that I'm pretty sure they're going to burst any moment. And that's without the aid of a pin.

"Seriously," I continue. "Thank you all so much. I really wasn't expecting this." The shower had been a complete surprise, with Nikki enlisting the help of her husband Damien to get me to the island by fabricating a crisis that needed my on-site attention. The island is the Resort at

Cortez, and it's fair to say this now-completed project was my first baby. A business venture that boosted me from the role of Damien Stark's executive assistant to project manager for Stark Real Estate Development.

Frankly, the resort turned out amazing. To say I'm proud would be an understatement.

"Come on, Sylvia. You sure you don't want to come out with us?" Jamie asks. She'd announced earlier that the entire group should go hit the club on the other side of the island for drinks and dancing. "The bartender makes a mean virgin strawberry daiquiri."

Beside her, Evelyn Dodge snorts. "Sweetie, none of us in this room are buying that you've ever come close to anything virgin. And besides," she adds, "I think our girl has somewhere else she'd rather be."

I smile gratefully at Evelyn. She's a Hollywood fixture, bold and brassy, and I've come to think of her as a pseudo-mom, especially during my pregnancy. Because god knows my own mother didn't even attempt to step up to the plate. "Evelyn's right," I say. "I just want to crash."

"Crash," Nikki repeats, with a knowing grin. "That's code for she wants to snuggle with Jackson."

I have to laugh. "It is," I admit. "It really is." I could pretend to be jealous that they're going to continue the party at the club, but I'm just not. I had a blast with my friends, but right now, I want my husband's arms around me.

"Then come on," Cass says. "Let's get you back to your bungalow safe and sound." She frowns at the doorway and the rain falling just past the porch. "I want to make sure you don't fall."

I roll my eyes. "I know how to walk, Cass."

"Hate to break it to you, but you don't walk anymore. You waddle."

I make a face, but I don't argue. Sadly, she's right. But as I rub my hand lightly over my huge belly, I can't deny that sore breasts and a pronounced waddle are a small price to pay for something as amazing as the child in my belly.

Jackson's child, I think, then let Cass hold my elbow to keep me steady as we start out toward my bungalow and the man I love.

Chapter Two

"CONGRATS AGAIN, MAN," Ryan Hunter said, giving Jackson a celebratory slap on the back as Blaine and Preston waited on the porch.

"Thanks." Jackson grinned. For that matter, he'd pretty much been grinning like an idiot all day. Why wouldn't he be? His wife was just weeks away from giving birth to his second child. Him, Sylvia, Ronnie, and the new baby—they made up an almost statistically perfect family. And considering the seriously screwed up family he'd grown up in, that alone was a miracle.

But what was even more of a miracle was the way he felt. Happy. Fulfilled. Even humbled that a woman like Sylvia was just as much in love with him as he was with her. They'd fought a long battle to get where they were now, but it was worth it.

Whatever he did for her was worth it.

Now, as he shut the door on the rain and his departing friends, he couldn't wait for the moment when she was back in his arms. She was only a short walk away—and she'd only been gone for a few hours—but during that span an ache had built in him that would only be soothed when he touched her. God, how he wanted to touch her. To kiss her lips. To taste the sweetness of her skin.

He wanted to rub his hand gently over her belly and feel the life inside. He wanted to bury himself inside her and know what the two of them, together, had created.

A miracle, that's for damn sure.

Most of all, he simply wanted to hold her.

With a sigh, he checked his watch, then reminded himself that it wasn't cool to call your wife's friends and tell them to hurry up with the baby shower. Instead, he poured himself another glass of scotch. It would be his fourth for the evening, but what the hell? After all, tonight had been a celebration for him, too. No pink and blue party favors, but it was still all about celebrating his growing family.

The soft sound of sheets rustling interrupted his thoughts, and he shifted automatically toward the baby monitor that sat on the pass-through to the kitchen, his lips curving into a smile as he pictured his four year old daughter, Ronnie, curled up in the sheet with Bun-bun, the newest member of her stuffed animal menagerie.

Yeah, he thought, as he glanced around the cozy living room. He'd been thoroughly domesticated.

And he absolutely loved it.

He might have been the one who designed this bungalow, just as he had all the other buildings on the island. But his wife and child were the ones who breathed life into these walls. Who made them a home just as much as their new house in the Pacific Palisades.

He took another sip of his scotch and started back to the couch, planning to grab his sketchbook and start working on the design of a playscape he'd been thinking about for their backyard. He didn't make it. Instead, he stopped, his entire body full of anticipation, the moment he heard footsteps on the patio followed by the sound of the doorknob turning, and then the increased volume of the rain as the front door swung open.

And then there she was—*Sylvia Brooks Steele.*

His wife.

And damn, but she took his breath away.

She didn't see him yet—her head was turned as she spoke to someone behind her. *Cass,* he realized, as he heard Syl's best friend say goodbye.

Then Syl turned back and stepped into the foyer. She closed the door behind her. And then, finally, she looked up and met his eyes and smiled so bright it seemed to Jackson that her entire body glowed.

"Hey," she said softly. "I missed you."

"Oh, baby," he said, as he moved to her and took her in his arms. "I've missed you, too."

I'M AS BIG as a house and haven't seen my feet in weeks. My breasts ache, my skin feels too tight for my body, and my lower back is a symphony of aches and pains, twinges and tweaks.

And yet despite all that, the moment I see him, I start to melt from the desire that floods through me. He's not doing anything other than standing in the living room looking at me. But even so, he's larger than life. That coal-black hair. Those ice blue eyes. The tall, straight posture that suggests he controls the room and everything—and everyone—in it.

Jackson Steele, the famous—some would say notorious—architect.

Jackson Steele, half-brother to tennis champion turned billionaire entrepreneur Damien Stark.

Jackson Steele, my husband, and the man who is the focal point of my world. Who grounds me and centers me. My white knight in so many ways.

It's astounding, really, how much I crave his touch. How turned on I get simply from looking at him. From knowing that he's mine. Granted, I've read all about pregnant women and their hormones, but this is more than that. This is a need that's burned within me from the first moment I saw him, and has only grown stronger since our wedding. Since I started to feel his child growing inside me.

I understand my desire—how could I not want this man? But what astonishes me is that even today, when I'm roughly the shape of a cantaloupe, I see the same expression on his face that I saw on our wedding night. He wants *me*, not just the packaging, and that knowledge warms me, making me feel safe and cherished.

Loved.

"You're wet," he says, coming to my side, and I have to laugh. Because he's right—I'm wet simply from looking at him. But I can tell from the tone of his voice that he's not talking about desire, but about my damp hair and shoulders. Not to mention the part of my belly that protruded out from the protection of the umbrella I was sharing with Cass.

He catches my reaction, of course, and I see the amused heat flash in his eyes even as his lips curve into a wicked grin. "I was going to suggest you put on some dry clothes, but now I'm thinking maybe you should just take those off."

"I could be convinced," I admit.

"I'm very glad to hear that," he says, as he comes closer and presses his hand over my belly. He moves toward me, his lips not yet reaching mine when a powerful kick makes us both jump, then laugh.

"I think he's awake," Jackson says.

"He? What makes you think it's a boy?" We'd decided not to find out the baby's sex, though I have to admit that there are times—like when I can't sleep and am shopping online at three a.m.—when I really wish I knew if I should be buying pink or blue.

"Must be a boy with a kick like that," Jackson says, earning a smack on his shoulder from me.

"Chauvinist," I say as he holds up his hands and laughs. "Speaking of strong women," I continue archly, "I assume Ronnie's asleep?"

"She stayed up long enough to be in charge of the chips for one round of poker and be thoroughly spoiled by all the guys. Then she started to get grouchy, so we called it a night. She's sound asleep with her bunny."

I frown, considering. "Maybe I should sneak it out of bed and wash it tonight? That thing has turned a shade of greenish-brown that really isn't natural."

"Better idea. Wash it tomorrow. Tonight, we can go peek at her from the doorway. Then I have other plans for you."

"Really? Like what, Mr. Steele?"

"For starters, a foot rub."

I practically swoon from the mere suggestion. Then I take his hand and lead him to the little bedroom at the opposite end of the hall from the master. The door is cracked open, and I can see the glow of golden light from her *Frozen* nightlight. I push it open slowly, then lean against Jackson as we both look at the dark-haired angel sleeping soundly, a bunny clutched against her chest, and her little thumb between her lips.

"I should get another blanket," I say, taking a step forward. Jackson's hand on my shoulder stops me.

"She'll just kick it off. That kid runs hot."

He's right, and I frown, annoyed at myself. "I know that. She hates having too many blankets. I just—"

"Want to take care of her. I know." He kisses the top of my head. "You're an amazing mom."

I sigh, and rest my head against his chest as I watch Ronnie sleep. "I hope so," I whisper, which is about as close as I can come to stating my fears. "With Ronnie—I don't know, it's like it's different since I stepped in later in the game."

"So did I," he says, and I nod, because he's right. Jackson had no idea he was a father for a long time, and even after he learned, Ronnie lived with her great grandparents for quite a while before he legally claimed paternity.

"True," I admit. "And I don't mean to sound all emotional and hormonal, really." I press my hands over my protruding stomach. "I mean, I'm so excited to meet this little person. But I'm still nervous. I just hope I'm half as good a mom as you are a dad. I'm at a disadvantage, you know," I say with a tease. "You've gotten the hang of this dad thing. I've only been a mom for a few months now."

"Almost nine months," he corrects me. "And that's if we only count the months since you adopted her. It's been about a year if we count the time you were Ronnie's mom in practice if not by law. Not that you needed the time. You were perfect from the moment you met her."

I wasn't—I was scared. Afraid I'd take after my own parents in the child-rearing department. The kind of parent that leaves scars on their children. Emotional scars that take a lifetime to heal, if they ever do.

But I'm not scared of that anymore. I'm not my dad. And I'm sure as hell not my mom. Now I'm just Sylvia. Very pregnant Sylvia with all the hopes and fears and insecurities of any pregnant woman.

In other words, a lot.

And, honestly, I'm sure Jackson must be a little nervous, too. After all, he's never actively parented an infant. For that matter, Ronnie must feel unsteady as well. She's outwardly excited about the baby, but I've seen signs of clinginess, and I'm sure that must be because a new sibling is coming.

"We should do something special for her," I say, looking at our sleeping princess. "Something just for Ronnie. Right about the time the baby's born, or just after."

He doesn't say anything for so long that I shift to see his face. I find him smiling, his expression gentle. "See?" he says. "You're a great mom."

"Just trying to think about what she needs."

"Exactly."

I turn in his arms, and tilt my head up for his kiss, soft and gentle on my lips. "Right now, though," I admit, "I'm going to be selfish and think about what I need."

"Oh? And what's that?"

"You. Beside me. In bed."

"Is that so?"

I answer by cupping the back of his head and pulling him down for another kiss. This one bold and so full of heat that I feel it coursing through me. Building and demanding.

And while I may have started it, he takes over fully, pulling me close so that my belly presses against him, and my breasts ache as he holds me tight against him. His hand slides down over my rear, and I moan a little because I want more.

I want Jackson.

He takes advantage of my little noises and urges my lips open, then deepens the kiss. I taste scotch and cigars, and smile against his kiss, thinking that the guys really had been doing their masters of the universe thing tonight.

When I finally break away, I'm breathing hard. "Make love to me, Mr. Steele."

"Mrs. Steele, it will be my pleasure."

Chapter Three

I'M SIMPLY DRESSED in a T-shirt and skirt, and now I sit on the edge of the bed to peel the skirt off, then just shift sideways, still half dressed. As I do, I get a rare glimpse of my ankles, so swollen I can't help but wince even though they don't hurt.

"Lie back," Jackson says. "I believe I promised you a foot massage."

He also promised me sex, but right at the moment, I want both pretty much equally. So I'm more than willing to settle back, close my eyes, and lose myself in the sensual bliss of being utterly pampered.

And blissful it is.

His touch is gentle but firm as he massages the soles of my feet, and it feels so good I actually whimper when he stops so that he can move his hands up and gently rub my swollen ankles. He does that for a while, and I expect him to stop, slide up my body, and kiss me.

Apparently Jackson has other plans.

Instead of stopping, he continues on by stroking my calves, the pressure rhythmic but firm, and I feel waves of tension leave my body as I pretty much turn to jelly.

"That's so nice," I say, my voice sounding far away and sleepy. But he doesn't answer. Instead, he gently tugs my legs apart and presses his lips to the soft skin of my right inner thigh, even while he gently strokes the left with the pad of his thumb.

He teases me, the tip of his tongue grazing lightly over my leg as he moves higher and higher, his hands on my thighs keeping me still despite the fact that I want to writhe with pleasure and anticipation. "Jackson!" I cry as he moves higher—as he's so very close, and I'm so very turned on. He says nothing in response, but his fingertip teases the edge of my panties, and I'm so turned on—so ready—that I gasp, then bite my lower lip, wanting his touch and yet so on fire that I'm not sure I'll be able to survive when he touches me more intimately.

"Jackson, please," I murmur, not sure if I'm begging him to stop or continue. It doesn't matter. He is relentless, and he runs the tip of his tongue between my thigh and pantyline even as he tugs the crotch of my underwear to the side, and I feel the rush of cool air mixed with his breath, and it's such a wonderfully decadent feeling that I almost go over right then.

I hear his murmur of satisfaction, and then I gasp and arch up as his mouth closes over me, his tongue teasing my clit, the pressure so right and perfect—and my body so damn primed and sensitive—that I can't hold it in any longer. Electricity shoots all the way through me, firing my skin, reducing me to ash as I shake and tremble and explode—all the while crying out the name of the man I love.

JACKSON HELD HIS BREATH, overwhelmed by the way Sylvia shattered in his arms, still awed by the knowledge that she was so completely his, and not just because of a wedding ring. And not even because of a child.

No, they were bound together by something stronger. Something primal.

Love. The real thing. The deepest, purest kind. And passion, too.

Together, they made a damn potent combination.

He grinned, thinking once again how lucky he was.

Beside him, Sylvia stretched. "Amazing." She practically purred, and the pleasure he took from seeing her satisfaction was just as powerful as if he'd orgasmed himself. "I'm completely limp. I think you destroyed me."

He chuckled. "Just so long as the destruction doesn't last."

"Mmm." She scooted closer, then bit her lower lip as she reached down to stroke his cock. He stiffened, and she looked up at him, her lids heavy. "Do you want—"

He hushed her with a gentle kiss. "I want to curl up next to my wife. I want to feel the press of your body against mine. And I want to hold you close while you fall asleep."

He could tell she wanted to protest on principle, but the exhaustion in her eyes stopped the words from coming. With a yawn, she rolled over, groaning a little as she moved with far less grace than usual. He didn't mention that, though. While he might be amazed and awed by every change in her, some things he'd learned to just keep quiet about.

After a moment, she was settled against the huge pillow

she'd been using since about her fifth month.

He eased closer, spooning against her back. "I didn't read to him tonight." He'd been reading *Alice in Wonderland.*

"Tomorrow," she said. "I think he's sleeping, anyway."

"You should, too."

Her answer was barely even a mumble. And as he rested his hand on her belly and thought about the small life within, the mother of his children fell asleep in his arms.

Chapter Four

"DO YOU NEED ME at the meeting on Monday?" Jackson asks Damien as we walk along the beach. I'm a few feet behind, walking silently beside Nikki, Cass, and Siobhan while they talk about the mobile app Nikki's designing for Cass's tattoo studio. The others had started out walking with us, but have either turned around or hung back to walk more slowly in the surf.

"Not necessary. We're not talking about the retail idea. Dallas said he wants to pitch me some new tech project," Damien adds, referring to Dallas Sykes, one of the resort's investors. He's one of the two heirs to the Sykes Department Store fortune and a rather notorious playboy. And the idea of him pitching a tech project just doesn't quite match my vision of the man who so often ends up on the wrong side of tabloid gossip.

Still, I'm glad Damien doesn't need Jackson at the meeting. We've planned to stay an extra day so that Ronnie can get more beach time, although I'm happy to have a day to do nothing but relax. Maybe it's the stress of getting to the island, or maybe it's too much fun at the shower last night—or with Jackson afterwards—but I haven't felt like myself all day. I'm draggy and a little nauseous and crampy. It's probably nothing—or just another lovely symptom that goes with pregnancy—but whatever the cause, I'm looking forward to pampering myself tomorrow with a day of total relaxation.

At least *I'll* be relaxing. I look ahead to where Ronnie's playing in the surf, racing back and forth to beat the waves up onto the sand, and can't help but be amazed by the fact that she's been going non-stop since we left the house.

As I watch, she stumbles and lands hard on her bottom. I immediately clutch my stomach, preparing to haul my girth over to her and make sure she's okay, but she just laughs and wiggles her toes in the incoming waves.

"Mommy! Look! I'm wet!"

I flash a grin toward Jackson as I walk at a more reasonable pace to her, already a little out of breath. "You certainly are. Wet and sandy."

"Can we build a castle? Pretty please?"

"That's your daddy's milieu," I say, the word making her frown. "I just mean that he designs and builds things."

She nods sagely. "He built this island."

I bite back my smile. "Well, the buildings on it, anyway." I hold out my hand for Jackson as he joins us. "Up for building a castle for your princess?"

"I don't see why not." And because he's an incredible father, he sits down in the wet sand without even thinking twice. "You guys go on ahead," he says to Damien. "Looks like I've been conscripted."

"Fair enough," Damien says. "An early dinner before the rest of us leave?"

Jackson nods. "We'll be there. Showered and sand

free." He ruffles Ronnie's hair. "Including this one."

"Bye, Uncle Damien! Bye, Aunt Nikki!"

"See you later, sweetheart," Nikki says, then blows her a kiss before continuing down the beach with Damien, Cass, and Siobhan.

Almost immediately, Ronnie leaps to her feet. "The water, Daddy! Wanna play in the water!"

"I thought you wanted to build a castle."

She nods vigorously. Apparently, the kid wants to do everything.

Jackson looks at me, helpless in the face of his daughter's wide eyes and bright smile. "What do you say? Want to play in the surf?"

I shake my head. "I'm going to sit here and watch her wear you out."

"Fair enough." He pulls me in for a kiss, which I enthusiastically return. Then, while he and Ronnie head into the water, I move slightly further down the beach to one of the free lounge chairs with a shade umbrella beside it.

I lay down and close my eyes, and the next thing I know Jackson is standing right over me.

"What?" I blink, confused. "I thought you were going to play in the surf with Ronnie."

His brow furrows. "Baby, it's been three hours."

My eyes fly open and I struggle to sit up. Jackson reaches down to help me, and I cling to him, both grateful and confused. "But—"

"Are you feeling okay?"

The concern is evident in his voice, and I rush to reassure him. "Just tired. I don't think I'm sleeping well. Your child has a tendency to kick, and it's hard to get comfortable. But I'm fine." I hold onto him as I stand up, and then almost fall when my knees go weak.

I manage a thin laugh. "Fine and slightly lightheaded."

"We're going back to the cabana and calling the doctor."

"She's going to tell me to eat something. I only had that smoothie for breakfast, and apparently that was a very long time ago." Early in my pregnancy I was consistently lightheaded, so he knows as well as I do that I just need to get some food in me.

"Then let's get you fed," he says, then calls Ronnie in from the water. She's having far too good a time, though, and begs for another hour. And when Jackson refuses, her mood shifts from pleasant to pouty.

"I can walk back myself," I tell him. "You can stay with her."

He shakes his head. "No. Both my girls need food and sleep. I'll call Damien and tell him we're eating at home."

Since I'm not in the mood for company, I don't argue. And when we get back, Jackson makes us both sandwiches and fruit, then tucks me on the couch with the television remote. "I'm going to go down to the dock and say goodbye. You're staying."

His tone makes it clear that there will be absolutely no argument. Normally, I'd argue anyway, but the fact is that I really am exhausted, and so I willingly agree.

"How about you?" he asks Ronnie. "Stay with Mommy or come with me?"

Since she's still annoyed with her dad for pulling her away from the surf, she climbs onto the couch and snuggles next to me. "Stay."

"Okay then." He ignores her mood, gives her a kiss, and then gives me a much more intimate one. "Back in thirty minutes."

"We're fine," I say. "Go. Tell everyone thanks again for me."

As soon as the door shuts behind him, I lift the remote to turn on the TV, but Ronnie's words stop me.

"Does the baby make you tired?"

I set the remote aside and consider the question. "Well, it's growing inside me. That means that my body has to work hard. So, yeah, in a way I guess the baby does make me tired."

She nods as if considering my answer.

"Do I make you tired, too? Is that why we came back?"

"Oh, no, sweetie. You don't make me tired. But I have to take care of myself for your little brother or sister. That's why your daddy wanted us to come back. To make sure I'm well and the baby's well."

"Am I well?"

"You're perfect."

I expect a smile, but instead I get a frown.

"Ronnie? Sweetheart, what's wrong?"

Her eyes dart to my belly. "Will you love it more?"

The question turns me cold. I know what it's like not to feel loved. To feel like the extraneous child. "No." I push the word out with all the force I can manage. "Absolutely not. I love you, Veronica, and I will always love you. Just like I'll always love the baby."

"But it's in your tummy. I wasn't ever in your tummy. So you have to love it more."

I force myself not to blink, because I cannot cry in

front of her. "Sweetie, no. No, that's not the way it works. I'm your mommy, and it doesn't matter that you weren't in my tummy. You're in my heart," I say, putting her hand over my chest. "You're in my heart, and I love you."

For a moment, she just sits there. Then she nods and snuggles close. I put my arm around her and exhale, wishing that Jackson were here to help me. To tell me that I did okay. That Ronnie's okay.

Is she okay?

After all, I know better than anyone how much fear and doubt a child can hide under the surface.

But what I don't know is how to make it all go away.

Chapter Five

"MORNING, SWEETHEART." AS SYLVIA sat up in bed, Jackson came in and put the tray over her. Toast and scrambled eggs since that seemed like an easy meal for breakfast in bed. Along with orange juice in a flute, which Sylvia liked to call a pregnant woman's mimosa.

"Morning? It's almost eleven. I can't believe you let me sleep so long."

"You were tossing and turning. I figured you could use a few extra hours." Honestly, he was surprised she got any sleep at all. She looked beautiful pregnant, but he knew she was getting damned uncomfortable.

"So just extra rest? This isn't part of a master plan to over-pamper me?"

"Is there such a thing?"

She tilted her head to the side and narrowed her eyes at him. "I'm starting to think so. And you need to stop worrying. I've felt fine since Sunday evening on the island. It's Tuesday morning now. I've done nothing but eat and bask and relax for thirty-six hours. You're spoiling me rotten."

She was right, of course. But the truth was he enjoyed

pampering her. "You have a problem with that?"

"Absolutely not." She finished her orange juice, then held out the glass. "More please."

He laughed, then left to get the carton. "Anything else, madam?" he asked when he returned and refilled her glass.

"I could use a kiss."

"Funny. So could I."

He put the orange juice on the side table, then bent over to brush his lips over his wife's. He'd intended a chaste kiss, but her lips parted, so soft and tempting that he had to taste her. And when she reached up and thrust her fingers in his hair and pulled him down, he felt himself grow hard. "I should cancel my conference call," he said when they broke the kiss, both breathing hard.

She shook her head. "For that project in DC? The hell you will." She took his hand, twining her fingers through his.

"What if you need me?"

"One, your office is attached to the house, so it's not like I'd have to go far to find you. And two, I'm fine, remember? Now you're just making excuses for sex."

"Trust me. I don't need any excuses for sex."

She laughed. "Good point. In that case, you can come right back and find me after the call."

"With incentive like that, it'll be a very short call."

"Good. It should be. After all, you're Jackson Steele. What else do they possibly need to know before they hire you?"

"I like the way you think. So what are you going to do while I'm off impressing the Washington elite?"

"I think I'll set Ronnie up on one side of the kitchen

table with her Play-Doh and me at the other and try to plow through all the emails that have built up over the last few days. I have a lot to take care of before I go on maternity leave." She bit her lower lip. "We're so close, Jackson. Can you believe it?"

Honestly, he could barely get his head around the thought. Soon there'd be a baby in the house. *Their* baby. "No," he said as he rubbed her stomach, imagining his son or daughter. "I really can't." He drew in a breath, then took her hand and held tight. "Two kids and a wife I adore. I don't know how the hell I got so lucky, but I know one thing. I wouldn't trade a single moment. Not for anything."

"I'M HUNGRY, MOMMY."

"What?" I'm preoccupied with a chain of emails between the city and my team about the placement of a sewer line on a Stark property outside of Palm Springs. "I'm sorry, baby. I didn't hear you."

"I'm hungry," she repeats as I look into her wide eyes from over the screen of my laptop.

"Okay, just give me two more minutes and I'll get you something."

"Hungry *now*."

"Veronica Steele, you just ate a whole bowl of strawberries less than half an hour ago. You can wait until I finish this." I keep my voice level and reasonable despite the fact that my head is throbbing from staring at crisis-filled emails for the last hour.

Her lower lip protrudes in a full-on pout that, even despite my headache, is pretty darn cute. Naturally, it takes all my effort to remain stern.

I turn back to my email, then hear the scrape of the chair as she gets down, goes to the water dispenser and fills a cup. She's behind me now, but I hear her step into the pantry, too, and assume we're out of napkins and she's gone in to get some.

When she returns to the table, I realize that I'm wrong. She has her water in one hand and a Chips Ahoy cookie in the other.

"Ronnie . . ."

"Hungry. I said I was."

"And I said I'd get you something to eat in two minutes. You can wait two minutes."

The lip pokes out again, and this time it's not so cute.

"I bet you won't make the baby wait."

My shoulders sag. "Oh, sweetie, come here."

She hesitates, then shuffles her feet forward. She's not paying enough attention though, and she runs into the table, and her water glass goes flying. And, dammit, I'm too ungainly to do anything about it. I can only awkwardly shove back from the table as water spills right on my computer keyboard.

"Ronnie!" I shout, not meaning to raise my voice, but I'm surprised and irritated and—I realize with some dismay—covered in spilled water along with my computer.

I look over and see the tears welling in her eyes and feel like an absolute bitch from hell. A bitch who certainly doesn't deserve to be a mom. "Oh, baby. I'm so sorry. You just startled me. I didn't mean to yell."

"I knew you liked the baby in your tummy better than me."

Her words slash through me, and I hear myself saying

no, no, as I reach for her. But she's gone, even her short legs too swift for me these days. The back door slams, and I lean over my destroyed laptop just long enough to mentally award myself the Worst Mother of the Year award.

Then I head toward the backyard, too.

I half consider getting Jackson, but I know this call is important, and they must be making progress since he's been on the phone for so long. Besides, this one is on me. I stroke my belly. "I can do this, can't I, sport?"

As if in response, the baby gives a gentle kick, as I hurry outside after Ronnie.

She's not hard to find. The yard is large, but only by Los Angeles standards. She's on the swing set that Jackson intends to replace with the massive playscape he's designing. One that can grow with the kids, even turning into a workout station when they're older.

I settle into the swing beside her, feeling more than a little precarious. But with my feet on the ground, I figure I'm okay. For a minute or two we just sit there saying nothing. Finally, I speak, but I look straight ahead, not at the little girl on a swing beside me. "Do you know I love Daddy?"

"Uh-huh."

"But I yell at him sometimes." I think back to some of the knock-down drag out fights I've had with Jackson. And then I smile when I think about making up.

"You do?"

"Sure," I say. "People lose their tempers, that doesn't mean they don't love you. But I shouldn't have gotten mad. I know it was an accident. I'm just feeling tired." I turn and look at her, and am thankful to see that she's looking back at me, not wary anymore. "And I feel very, very big, too. Do you want to know a secret?"

She nods.

"This baby growing in my tummy is making me a little cranky."

She licks her lips. "I think you look pretty."

"And I think you're sweet."

Her smile widens.

"Can I tell you another secret?" I ask.

"Okay."

"I'm kind of nervous. I've never had a baby before. I really wish I'd been your mommy when you were little, but I'm so glad I have you now. Especially since I don't really know what I'm doing. And I'm going to need you to help me. After all, that's what big sisters do, right?"

"You really want me to?"

"Are you kidding? You're going to be just about the most important person in this baby's life."

"Me?"

"Absolutely, you. So will you help me?"

She nods. "I promise."

"Still hungry? How does mac and cheese sound?"

When she nods again, I start to get up, but a stabbing paining my middle has me doubling over and falling from the swing's seat into the sand.

"Mommy!"

I'm breathing hard, pain radiating through me. "Daddy," I manage to say. "Go get Daddy."

Her eyes are wide, and she's frozen.

"For me," I manage to croak. "For your little brother or sister."

"Brother," she says. "I wanna be the only little girl."

"We'll see." I smile despite the pain. "Now, go."

She does, racing across the lawn, her feet churning, her little lungs shouting *Daddy!* louder than I would have believed she could manage.

And then I don't see her anymore. Just gray. Just pain.

Nothing at all until I see Jackson racing toward me, and Ronnie coming up fast behind him.

Then there's a strange rushing in my ears, and it's not until Jackson reaches my side that I realize it's a helicopter.

"We're taking you to the hospital," he says, and even my fear isn't enough to ground me. I feel his arms. I feel my tears.

And after that, I don't feel anything at all.

Chapter Six

JACKSON PACED THE HOSPITAL hallway as he ended the call, not sure what he'd just told Nikki, but hoping that he'd made some sort of sense to her.

But the nurse was there now, standing in front of him, telling him that Sylvia was doing okay. She was calling for him, and they'd let him in the second they could.

Then she hurried back into the room and he was left standing there taking deep breaths and forcing himself to stay calm. He couldn't lose the baby. Christ, he couldn't lose Sylvia.

He was functioning right now, but only because he had to. He had to be strong for Ronnie. And he couldn't give in to his fear. But he was afraid—so damn afraid.

She'd been unconscious for the entire trip to the hospital. Worse, there'd been blood. Not much, but enough to rip him to shreds. His wife. His child. And oh, god, he might lose them both. And he hadn't been able to do a goddamn thing except curse the helicopter for being too slow and the universe for being a bitch.

It had been worse because he hadn't known anything. The paramedics did their job—he would give them that—

but they couldn't tell him anything concrete. Only that he had to talk to the doctors. Only that he had to wait.

He was still waiting.

No. He at least knew the situation now. Knew that they had her stabilized. Knew that they were doing what they could for her and for the baby.

But was it enough?

Oh, dear god, it had to be enough.

He drew in a breath, the doctor's words a jumble in his head. All Jackson had really understood was that Syl had gone into early labor. That wasn't a bad thing in and of itself, but the cord was around the baby's neck, and she was too far along for a C-section. As for the bleeding and the way she passed out—well, that was something Jackson couldn't wrap his mind around. But he knew from the doctor's expression—and from the fact that they wouldn't let him in the goddamn room—that it was serious.

Oh, Christ. Oh, Christ.

"Daddy?"

He sank down onto the couch and pulled Ronnie to him, hugging her tight, taking some small comfort in the feel of his daughter in his arms.

"I'm sorry."

Something in her voice told him that she wasn't just sympathizing with him, but that she was apologizing. "Sorry? Sweetie, what are you sorry for?"

Big tears fell from her eyes to plop on her jeans. "It's my fault. 'Cause I wanted to be the baby. And 'cause I made Mommy mad and that hurt her tummy."

"*No*." He pulled her close, then hugged her tight. "Baby, you didn't do anything bad." If anything, he should have insisted she go to the hospital because she'd been feeling so tired. Maybe if he had...

He shook the thoughts away. No time for self-recrimination now. He had to be strong for Syl. For Ronnie. For the baby.

He held tight to his daughter's arms, focused on her face, wanting her to understand. "You're the one who got her help, remember? That's good, baby. You did really, really good."

He couldn't tell if she was convinced or not, but as he started to ask her another question he saw the nurse hurrying toward him. He leaped to his feet, clutching Ronnie's hand as he did. "Syl," he demanded. "The baby."

His chest was too tight to get out any other words. All he could do in the infinity that stretched out before she answered was wait and hope.

"It's okay. They're fine. Your wife and your baby are fine."

He'd never felt such a palpable relief. The way it swept through him, taking every bit of strength with it, as if he'd used it all up fighting to stay steady. He reached out, grabbing the wall with his free hand so that he wouldn't tumble to the ground, and by sheer will alone he managed to right himself.

"They're okay? Really?"

The nurse's expression lit up. "I promise, Mr. Steele. They're fine." She swept her hand toward the door, and then reached down for Ronnie. "What do you say we go first? Show your daddy that your mommy and baby brother are doing just fine."

Brother.

"I have a son?" Jackson asked, as the nurse looked up at him, beaming, her smile just about lighting the hallway.

"Yes, Mr. Steele. You have a son."

"MOMMY!"

I'm exhausted and sore and I don't think I've ever been happier as I hold my son while my daughter skips toward my bed, Jackson behind her looking as tired and as happy as I feel. As if he's been through a battle zone, and come out victorious on the other side.

But then again, he has. And it would have been worse for him. I was occupied by the pain and the doctors. And now, all the manipulations they did to my body, are fading thanks to the lingering effects of the drugs, leaving me with a happy afterglow and a baby in my arms.

But Jackson had been out in that hall all alone without a clue as to what was happening even though I had begged for him to be with me.

They'd refused, pissing me off in the process. But now that the baby is here and he's safe, I have to admit I'm pretty much willing to forgive anything.

Now, Ronnie scrambles up onto the bed, and I do my best not to wince. She leans over me and peers at the tiny boy in the blue blanket. Jackson stands at the bed, too, and though I expect him to say something, all he does is look at me and our baby with an expression that is as close to rapture as I've ever seen.

"Is that my brother?"

"That's him," I say. "All six pounds four ounces of him."

"I'm sorry, Mommy."

I use my free hand to push her hair off her face. "You don't have a thing to be sorry about. You were absolutely perfect, and I love you desperately. In fact," I add with a sly grin, "you're my very favorite daughter."

She giggles. "I love you, Mommy."

"I know you do, sweetie."

"Can I still help with the baby?"

"You better," I say. "I need your help, just like I told you. I have a feeling this little guy is going to keep us busy." I glance up at Jackson. "He's a fighter," I say. "A survivor."

He nods, and I watch as his face comes alive and his smile breaks free. "He takes after his mom," he says softly, his voice breaking only at the end. "Oh, god, Syl. I thought—"

I shake my head and reach for his hand. "No. Please. Everything's good." I glance at the baby. "Perfect, even."

"Perfect," Jackson repeats.

"Do you want to hold him?" I ask, and Jackson reaches down very gently to pick up the precious bundle. He peers at our son's tiny face, then inspects the little fingers. When he looks back at me, his expression is full of awe.

"Do you know how much I love you?"

"Of course I do," I say. "I always have."

We stay that way for what feels like forever, lost in each other's eyes, our newborn son between us. Then Ronnie bounces on the bed, breaking the spell and making me laugh.

"What's his name, Daddy? What's his name?"

Jackson looks at me, for confirmation before saying, "Jeffery Michael Steele." And he says it with such firm authority that I wonder how we could have ever debated any others. Because that is so very clearly our little boy's name.

"Welcome to the family, Jeffery," I say.

"We love you," Ronnie adds, clutching my hand. I squeeze hers tight, my eyes on Jackson and our son.

I yawn and my eyelids droop as exhaustion takes its toll. It has, after all, been a very long day.

And then, finally, I drift off to sleep, surrounded by the three people I love most in all the world, and knowing that tomorrow, a new kind of adventure begins.

The End

Don't miss *Anchor Me*, the fourth book in The Stark Trilogy!

Check out all of JK's books at www.jkenner.com

J. Kenner (aka Julie Kenner) is the *New York Times*, *USA Today*, *Publishers Weekly*, *Wall Street Journal* and #1 International bestselling author of over seventy novels, novellas and short stories in a variety of genres.

JK has been praised by *Publishers Weekly* as an author with a "flair for dialogue and eccentric characterizations" and by *RT Bookclub* for having "cornered the market on sinfully attractive, dominant antiheroes and the women who swoon for them." A five-time finalist for Romance Writers of America's prestigious RITA award, JK took home the first RITA trophy awarded in the category of erotic romance in 2014 for her novel, *Claim Me* (book 2 of her Stark Trilogy).

In her previous career as an attorney, JK worked as a lawyer in Southern California and Texas. She currently lives in Central Texas, with her husband, two daughters, and two rather spastic cats.

Visit JK online at www.jkenner.com

Made in the USA
Lexington, KY
24 March 2017